Francis McCarten

In Peace and in War

Francis McCarten

In Peace and in War

ISBN/EAN: 9783337224936

Printed in Europe, USA, Canada, Australia, Japan

Cover: Foto ©Andreas Hilbeck / pixelio.de

More available books at **www.hansebooks.com**

DESCRIPTION

AND

CRUISE

OF THE

U. S. S. "AUGUSTA,"

SOUTH-ATLANTIC BLOCKADING SQUADRON.

ENOCH G. PARROTT,

Commander.

H. L. HOWISON,
Lieut. & Ex. Officer.

BY
FRANCIS McCARTEN,
1876.

PREFACE.

In introducing this little work to my friends and the public, I do not fear criticism, as my object has simply been to lay before them a few pleasing and interesting reminiscences of nearly seven years in the U. S. Navy, 1861 to 1864, 1875 to 1878.

My description of places and events are necessarily somewhat brief—but I trust on that account none the less interesting, as they are confined to facts merely, and are derived from the best authenticated sources only.

I do not attach any pecuniary value to this undertaking, but it has been throughout my earnest wish in these few sketches to excite a kind and sympathetic interest among my fellow voyages across the trackless ocean, and enable them by this means to record some of our adventures to the "Old Folks at Home." Trusting my endeavors to please may be crowned with success.

I am your obedient servant,

F. McCarten.

HAMPTON ROADS.

The AUGUSTA left New York, October 1861, for Hampton Roads, where an expedition was fitting out under command of Brig. General T. W. SHERMAN. The expedition was to sail to its destination under convoy of a naval squadron, commanded by Commodore DUPONT. The fleet consisted of eighteen men-of-war and thirty-eight transports. The transports were ordered to move in three columns, in the rear of their armed protectors. The sailing vessels were to be towed by the steamers. Surf boats were provided, sufficient to land three or four thousand men at once. Six hundred sailors were selected to manage the boats.

OFF CAPE HATTERAS

On Tuesday, October 29th, the squadron put to sea, none but the commanding officers knowing wheather it was bound. When three days out, and off Cape Hatteras, we encountered a terrific gale, which so utterly dispersed the fleet, that on Saturday morning, from the deck of the "AUGUSTA," the Flag-ship WABASH only was in sight. The next day the gale abated, and the ships began to reappear. As they came together, they had many disasters to report. The gun-boat ISAAC SMITH, to escape from foundering, was compelled to throw overboard a valueable battery. The transport PEERLESS, in a sinking condition, succeeded in placing her people on board the MOHICAN. The steamer GOVORNER went down, after the SABINE had, by heroic exertions, saved all on board. On Monday, November the 4th, the WABASH, AUGUSTA, and twenty-three others, came to anchor outside the bar at Port Royal, a magnificent harbor, on the South Carolina coast, about fifty miles south of Charleston.

PORT ROYAL.

The rebels had removed all the buoys from the channel. The little Surveying steamer VIXEN, immediately went to work and buoyed out the channel. That night all the light-draught vessels were anchored inside the bar. A few rebel steamers under COM. TATNALL, appearing in sight, the gun-boats opened upon them, and chased them under the guns of a battery which guarded the entrance of the harbor. The mouth of the harbor called Broad River, is about two and a half miles wide. Upon the south shore which is called Hilton Head, there was a formidable battery of twenty-three guns. On the north shore, which is called Bay Point, there was two batteries one mounting fifteen and the other four guns.

The outside bar was two miles wide, and in crossing it at high tide the keel of the WABASH would come within a foot of the bottom. The passage of this frigate over the bar was watched with intense anxiety, and when the feat was accomplished, cheers burst from the whole fleet. The other large ships immediately followed, and at once prepared for action. But a rising gale, and other unavoidable causes of detention, rendered it necessary to delay the assault, upon the forts until the next day. It was however, judged best to send out a reconnoissance of a few gun-boats, to draw the fire of the batteries, that their situation and strength might be ascertained.

RECONNOITERING.

Early Tuesday morning, the tug-boat Mercury ran along the sand beach skirting Hilton Head. One or two other armed vessels were creeping cautiously along the suspicious shores. It was a beautiful morning, the serene sky, the mirrored bay, and the soft, luxuriant outline of the land presented an aspect of rare loveliness. For an hour the sail seemed to be but a delightful pleasure excursion. But about half past seven the batteries on Hilton Head and Bay Point opened upon the adventurous explorers, and for two hours there was a fierce conflict, our object was to ascertain the position of the rebel batteries, and the number and weight of their guns. Com. TATNALL, now a rebel officer, but had grown gray in our service, led his fleet of rebel gun-boats, against the flag he should have defended with his life. The object of the reconnoissance having been attained, a signal from the flag-ship recalled the gun-boats.

The rebels, seeing our vessels retire, thought they were defeated, though, in reality, they had not received the slightest harm. The petty little fleet of rebel gun-boats followed them, when two or three of our gun-boats turned and hurled upon them such volleys of shot and shell, that they wheeled about and scampered back into the creeks, which excited a general burst of laughter.

On Wednesday, for some unexplained reason, no attack was ordered, and though doubtless vigorous preparations were being made for the great battle, the day seemed to be passed in inaction. The morning of Thursday dawned beautiful and clear, and as mild as the most balmy day in June. The groves, on the shore, were vocal with the songs of birds, and butterflies were flitting about through the rigging of the ships. The scene presented as the sun rose from the wave, was one of the most charming which can be imagined. The placid bay, the luxuriant shores, the distant ocean, the frowning forts, the majestic frigates and war steamers, scowling defiance upon the foe we were about attacking, and the fleet of defenseless transports anchored at a safe distance, upon whose deck and rigging an army of fifteen thousand men were clustered, waiting for the opening of one of the sublimest tragedies of war—all this presented a panorama of life and beauty, such as few eyes have beheld.

LINE OF BATTLE.

The plan of the battle was admirable in its simplicity and efficiency. The ships, forming in line steamed in a circle very slowly, each one as it entered the mouth of the river, about two and a half miles wide, delivering incessant broadsides upon Fort Beauregard, and the battery on Bay Point, and as it turned and came out upon the other shore, pouring the same deadly volleys into Fort Walker upon Hilton Head. This circle was about two and a half miles in its longest diameter, and three-quarters of a mile in its shortest. There were fifteen ships comprising this circle, mounting in all 145 heavy guns.

THE BALL OPENED.

It was a beautiful sight as this fleet swept into line, so silent, soon to burst into the loudest thunders, and the most desolating storm of war. This wicked rebellion has often arrayed brother against brother, and father against son. In this case brother was arrayed against brother.

At 10 o'clock the action commenced, the first three shots being fired from the rebel fort upon the flag-ship which led the advance. The tremendous response of the WABASH consisted of two entire broadsides from he two batteries of twenty-six guns each, and from her pivot gun. She steamed along as slowly as possible, only fast enough to give her steerage way. These immense guns were loaded and fired each one every minute. Fifty-three guns a minute, for twenty minutes, was the incessant peal from that one ship alone. But the other ships following on, came gradually into range and opened their fire. The ships ran within five hundred yards of the batteries, and threw their shot and shell with a force which would make them efficient at a distance of two and a half miles.

DISMOUNTING THEIR GUNS.

Many of the enemies guns were large columbiads, throwing one hundred and thirty pound shot. In less than twenty minutes, three of these cannon were dismounted. By the plan of attack seven or eight vessels were able to play upon the rebel batteries at the same time, each commencing as soon as it arrived within three-fourths of a mile of the forts, and continuing until three-fourths of a mile beyond. The fleet of JOSIAH TATNAL, had already been treated so roughly by the few gun-boats which conducted the reconnoissance, and was so appalled by the tremendous fire of the whole fleet, that it ran away into the distant inlets. When the whole of our fleet was in operation, fifty of the most terrible projectiles, round shot and shell, fell upon each of the forts, as the ships passed every minute. As each ship held the fort for twenty minutes within its range every time the line came around, which was at very short intervals, 400 of these projectiles fell upon the fort.

The explosion of one of these shells in the midst of a group of men is awful beyond description. The fragments are hurled in all directions, tearing perhaps a score of human bodies to pieces, and hurling the remains, mingled with earth and guns through the air. When a 32-pound shot strikes a man but little of him remains. Even the concussion of the air, when such a shot passes near, knocks one down.

After a short time, while the main body of the fleet continued to move in its circle, four of the gun-boats were sent to a position where they could rake Fort Walker. The gun-boat POCAHONTAS, Capt. PERCIVL DRAYTON, now came in from sea, on hearing the bombardment, and took his position to sweep Fort Walker with his guns, though his brother was in command of that fortification.

CEASE FIRING.

A little after noon the signal " cease firing " was made from the flagship, and the steamers swept beyond the reach of the batteries to rest the men and give them some refreshments, before returning to their exhausting work. On board the AUGUSTA we "spliced the main-brace" snatched a a hard-tack and returned to our quarters. The rebel fleet, and several other steamers crowded with spectators, that came down from Charleston to witness the defeat of our vessels, lay silently watching the movements of our fleet, when the author of this sketch by permission of his superior officer trained his gun a rifled howitzer stationed on the forecastle, and having removed the elevation screw so as to give the gun extreme elevation fired, and after waiting for several seconds had the pleasure of seeing it drop right in the midst of the rebel fleet, which caused them to scatter in all directions amidst shouts of laughter from the whole fleet.

The perfect confidence with which the rebels had commenced the fight was suddenly changed to utter consternation. The bolts of death fell upon them so mercilessly and incessantly, that in mortal terror, simultaneously they droped their arms and fled, leaving everything behind them—their coats which they had thrown off, their watches, their money, costly swords —all the treasures of the camp.

THE FLIGHT.

The flight of the garrison was seen by the thousands who crowded the transports, and a shout of delight arose, even louder than the voices of the artillery. Capt. Rogers, from the WABASH, was sent with a flag of truce to the shore, to ascertain if the flight were real or a feint. The fort was found entirely deserted not a living being in it. The Stars and Stripes were immediately run up upon the ramparts, thus announcing to the fleet that the insulted Goverment, in its majesty, had again planted its foot upon the soil of rebellious South Carolina.

The firing ceased, cheers of almost frantic joy burst again and again from thousands of lips; the bands on the various ships pealed forth, over the still waters, the imposing strains of Yankee Doodle and the Star Spangled Banner. The action lasted five hours.

LANDING THE TROOPS,

Measures were immediately adopted for landing the soldiers. The Connecticut 7th, in twenty-seven large boats, were pulled to the beach, and almost at the same instant 1.046 men sprang upon the beach. Pickets were thrown out in all directions, a double guard set, and every precaution adopted against surprise. But the terror stricken rebels had fled, with no thought but to escape from the terrible bombardment. Their tents, outside the fort, were were filled with luxuries. One of the soldiers found $1,000 in gold and silver. In the forts and batteries there were about 1,800 men. The guns were found to be mostly 130 pound columbiads, of admirable finish, and the forts were on the most appro ved plan of military engineering. The whole land force of the expedition was soon transferred to the shore, and the fortifications, on both sides of the river, were seized and garrisoned by our troops. An act of treachery, was here discovered. The rebel flag at Bay Point, which fort the rebels left quite deliberately when the found that Fort Walker was taken, was fixed as a snare, so that, when our men should attempt to haul it down, it would explode a percussion cap, which would fire the magazine. By some accident the train of powder had been broken. And though the cap exploded and fired the train, the interupted communication with the magazine saved hundreds from destruction. Nearly all the rebels escaped, twenty-five only were taken prisoners, who were sick in the hospitals.

Fifty large cannon, three hundred muskets, the entire camp equipage of three regiments, fell, with the forts, into our hands. Our loss was but eight killed and twenty-five wounded. The loss of the rebels 120 killed and 100 wounded.

The AUGUSTA had been during the fight a conspicuous target for the rebel guns. She was struck several times in the hull and rigging. The WABASH was struck twenty-five times. The BIENVILLE was struck five times. The PENGUIN was struck upon the steam chest and disabled, she was taken in tow by the AUGUSTA. All the ships were more or less wounded. The rebels had probably no idea that our ships would venture up to the very muzzles of their guns, and their guns were accordingly sighted for a range of one or two miles. The most of their shot passed through the rigging. And when the bombardment commenced, and shells were rained down upon the forts at the rate of fifty a minute, the confusion was too great to admit of careful aim.

Our ships were kept continually in motion. Probably there was never an engagement of such magnitude, where a fleet was exposed to so heavy a fire, with so slight a loss. When we reflect that the immense columbiads of the rebels were in such a position, that fifty could be brought to bear upon each ship, it does seem strange that any one of the fleet could have escaped destruction.

Among the incidents of the battle, a hundred and thirty pound shot, after ricochetting four times, bounded directly over the Bienville, and plunged into the Augusta. William Steele, a boy fourteen years of age, served at one of the guns, as "powder monkey," with composure which excited astonishment, never flinching or dodging a shot. And when two men fell dead, torn to pieces at the gun, he stepped carefully over the bodies, and continued in the discharge of his duty as if nothing had happened. Thomas Jackson, coxwain of the Wabash, had his leg torn off, so that it hung only by a small portion of the muscle and skin. Deliberately he took out his knife, and endeavoured to cut the limb off. The knife was so dull that, though he sawed manfully, he could not sever the limb. He was taken below, and died in two hours, saying that he was happy to suffer for the "dear old flag."

From our whole fleet, 3,500 shot and shell were thrown into and upon the forts. It had been carefully estimated that the average value of each shot delivered at the forts was eight dollars. The whole cost of the five hours' fight was about $ 28,000, and the whole money cost to the Goverment could not have been less than five million of dollars.

The Army was put in possession of Port Royal, where it remained to the close of the war, in inaction, and was used as a refugee camp, thousands of negro's flocked to this point, and was kept in idleness, at the expense of the Goverment, school teachers were sent from the New-England States, to educate those freed slaves.

This victory created the wildest enthuiasm throughout the North. The national flag had been planted on the traitorous soil of South Carolina, never to be displaced till every stronghold of the state was in our possession. Our ill-successes on land thus far had been a cause of deep mortification, and this first great essay of the navy recalled to mind the halo of glory it hung around the nation during the first year of the second war with England, when successive defeats on land made the people's cheeks crimson with shame. Whenever one met a naval man the eye of the latter brightened, and with a proud shake of the head he would say, "I told you how it would be when the 'blue jackets' got a chance." "Ah we are all sure of the navy," was the common remark. It is said that Commodore Barron, then a prisoner in Fort Warren, when he read a descripton of the fight, and how gallantly his old ship, the Wabash, bore herself, forgot he was a rebel prisoner, and exclaimed, "By heavens! OUR navy can beat the world."

Immediately after the capture of Port Royal, the Augusta was ordered to blockade the entrance to the Savannah River. While lying off this place we captured the ship Cheshire of Liverpool, while trying to run the blockade.

TYBEE ISLAND.

In the month of November, we made a reconnoissance in the direction of Tybee Island, at the mouth of the Savannah river, as a preliminary to the reduction of Fort Pulaski, which commands the approaches to Savannah Georgia. Savannah is one of the most beautiful of the Southern Cities, containing a population of about 6,000 whites and 6,000 slaves. Tybee Island, is a low, barren expanse of sand ridges, about eight miles long and six wide. At the northern extremity of the island there is a light-house and what is called Martello Tower, supposed to one of those massive circular structures of masonry, such as the English scattered so profusely along their coasts to guard against the threatned invasion by Napoleon, but in reality was built of mud and sea-shells. On the 25th, of November, the Augusta, Flag, and Pocahontas, got under weigh and steamed in the direction of Tybee Island, and commenced throwing shell in the direction of the battery without receiving any response. Immediately Captain Parrott, of the Augusta, hoist the signal "arm & equip boats." The boats were lowered and manned and immediately pulled for the beach, where we were drawn up in line of battle on the shore, and the order given to "charge," up the beach we went in the direction of the fort, on arriving there we found it entirley deserted. It has often been remarked that as soon as a company of sailors land on the beach, it is pretty hard to keep them together, after the order "charge" is given. In less time than it takes to tell it, they were scattered in all directions all over the island, the woods, dwellings, light-house and every place where a rebel might be lurking were searched in vain. While one of my companions and myself were exploring the light-house, and on reaching the top, found the flag-staff still remained, but the halyards was unrove. I went immediately and procured a flag from one of our boats and bent it on to a long pole and succeeded in placing it out of the upper window, when cheer after cheer went up from our men all over the island, in sight of Pulaski, who opened fire on us.

Fort Pulaski is situated at the mouth of the river, on a small island called cockspur, and perfectly commands the approaches in every direction. The rebels felt that they had at least one fort, Pulaski, which was impregnable. Our men immediately commenced throwing up intrenchments, and mounted one of our guns on the tower. A guard was kept on shore night and day until the army under Gen. Gillmore, arrived from Port Royal, and took possession of the island, which afterwards reduced Fort Pulaski.

Just twelve months to a day, from the time when the rebels took possession of Sumter, Pulaski, surrendered to the Union forces under Gen. Hunter and Com. Rodgers, of the Wabash. Three hundred and eighty-three prisoners. The rebel officers surrendered their swords to Major Halpine, (Private Miles O'Reilly.)

The Augusta was ordered to the blockade off Charleston, S. C., where her crew was engaged in sinking the "stone fleet" in the channel, and after taking off their crews, and saving everything that could be of any value to the Goverment; and also having on board a number of prisoners, taken from blockade runners, we proceeded to Philadelphia. After receiving some slight repairs, and an addition to our battery, we left for Hampton Roads, in the month of Feb. where an Expedition was fitting out under Gen. B. F. Butler, and the brave old warrior Farragut, in his flag-ship the Hartford—a vessel destined to assume a prominent place in this little book, and second to none in the annals of history, not even excepting the old "Constitution." The place of rendezvous was Ship Island, at which we arrived in seventeen days. The Augusta was not the class of vessel which Farragut wanted for reducing the batteries on the Mississippi, being too great a target for the enemies guns. She was then ordered back to Charleston, and on the passage North, called at Havana, and Key West, received information of the capture of the steamship Ariel, by the Alabama. We were immediately sent out in search of the Pirate, and also to convoy two steamers from Aspinwall, to New York, the "America," and "Champion." Having performed this duty we returned to the blockade of Charleston, where we remained until the morning of January 31. 1863.

ENGAGEMENT WITH THE REBEL RAMS.

At about 4 25 this morning, two iron clad rams, from Charleston, in the obscurity of a thick haze, and the moon having just set, succeeded in passing the bar, near ship channel, unperceived by the squadron, and made an attack upon the Mercedita. Her Captain says:

At 3 A. M., we had slipped cable and overhauled a troop steamer, running for the channel by mistake, At 4, I laid down. Lieut. Commander Abbott was on deck giving orders to Acting Master Dwyer about recovering the anchor, when they saw a smoke and the faint appearance of a vessel close at hand. I heard them exclaim, "She has black smoke;" watch, " man the guns," "spring the rattle," " call all hands to quarters." Mr. Dwyer came to the cabin door. telling me a steamboat was close aboard. I was then in the act of getting my pea jacket, I sang out, "train your guns right on him and be ready to fire as soon as I order." I hailed "Steamer ahoy! Steer clear of us and heave-to. What steamer is that?" Then ordered my men " Fire on him." Told him, " You will be into us. What steamer is that?" His answer to first or second hail was "Hallo!" The other replies were indistinct, either by intention or from being spoken inside of his mail armor, until in the act of striking us with his prow, when he said. "This is the Confederate States steam ram." I repeated the order, "Fire! Fire!" but no gun could be trained on him, as he approached on the quarter, struck us just abaft our aforemost 32-pound gun, and fired a heavy rifle through us diagonally, penetrating the starboard side through our Normandy condenser, the steam-drum of port boiler, and exploding against port side of ship, blowing a hole in its exit some four or five feet square.

The vessel was instantly filled and enveloped with steam. Reports were brought to me, "Shot through both boilers," "fires put out by steam and water," "gunner and one man killed, and a number of men fatally scalded, water over fire-room floor, vessel sinking fast." "The ram has cut us through at and below the water-line on one side, and a shell has burst at the other almost at water-edge."

After the ram struck, she swung around under our starboard counter, her prow touching, and hailed, "Surrender, or I'll sink you! Do you surrender?" And after receiving reports, I answered, " I can make no resistance; my boiler is destroyed." " Then, do you surrender?" I said, " Yes;" having found my moving power destroyed, and that I could bring nothing to bear but muskets against his shot-proof coating.

He hailed several times to send a boat, and threatned to fire again. After some delay, a boat was lowered, and Lieut. Commander Abbott asked if he should go in her, and asked for orders what to say. I told him to ask what they demanded, and to tell him the condition we were in.

He proceeded on board, and, according to their demand, gave his parole on behalf of himself and all the officers and crew. The ram having been detained half an hour or more, ran out for steamer Keystone State. The firing then receded to northward and eastward, and was pretty brisk at the head of the line.

THE KEYSTONE STATE.

The Keystone State, commanded by Le Roy, was also disabled, and claimed as a prize by the rebels. The details of the fight thus given by her commander:

Satisfied, from the view obtained through my night glasses, that the steamer was a ram, I ordered the starboard bow gun fired at her, which was at once responded to by a shot from the stranger, when I ordered the starboard battery fired as soon as the guns could be brought to bear, putting the helm aport. On heading to the northward and eastward, discovered a ram on either quarter. Soon after the first gun, fire was reported forward below. After extinguishing it, fire was again reported in the same place, when the ship was kept off seaward to enable us to put out the fire and get things in a condition to attack the enemy. Odered full steam, and about daylight discovered black smoke and stood for it, for the purpose of running her down, exchanging shots rapidly with her, striking her repeatedly, but making no impression, while every shot from her was striking us. About 6.17 A. M., a shell, entering on the port side, forward of the forward guard, destroyed the steam chimneys, filling all the forward part of the ship with steam. The port boiler emptied of its contents, the ship gave a heel to starboard, nearly down to the guard, and the water from the boiler, and two shot -holes under water, led to the impression the ship was filling and sinking, a foot and a half of water being reported in hold. Owing to the steam, men were unable to get supplies of ammunition from forward. Ordered all boats ready for lowering. Signal-books thrown overboard, also some small arms. The ram being so near, and the ship helpless, and the men slaughtered by almost every discharge of the enemy, I ordered the colors to be hauled down, but finding the enemy were still firing upon us, directed the colors to be rehoisted and resume our fire from the after-battery. Now the enemy, either injured or to avoid the squadron approaching, sheered off towards the harbor.

The Augusta had slipped her cable but remained in her position, all hands were to quarters, not even a whisper were to be heard all through the ship. Now the haze began to clear away, and the daylight fast approaching, discovered black smoke and the ship was headed in the direction of the stranger, taking her to be a blockade runner we headed for her with the intention of cutting her off from the channel, but on coming closer found her to be a ram, swung the ship around and fired, our shots bounding off her like so many beans without doing her any injury, while every shot she fired went clear through us, making the splinters fly in all directions. One of our hundred-pound rifle shots struck her pilot-house carrying away the flag-staff. The other ram fired a few shots and ran in for the channel, we followed as far as the depth of water would allow us.

During all this time the Housatonic remained at anchor, she being the only naval built vessel in the squadron, and would be like'y to give them a good brush, but did not engage them until they got in over the bar, then commenced firing at long range.

Gen. Beauregard issued a proclamation declaring the blockade destroyed, and that foreign governments should so regard it. The pompous manifesto was not regarded by Com. Dupont, and the blockade was continued. The New Iron-Sides, came from Port Royal that night, and there was no more rams to be seen outside of Sumter after that.

THE IRON-CLADS ATTACK ON SUMTER.

This fleet was composed of nine vessels, and placed under the command of Admiral Dupont. Having rendezvoused in Port Royal, and sailed from there on the 1st of April, 1863, to try the great experiment of the century, and the next day arrived at Edisto. The water over Charleston bar not being of sufficient depth in ordinary times to float them, the heavy spring tides of April, was selected for the passage of the vessels. On Sunday morning at daybreak the fleet moved out to sea, and in a few hours lay off Charleston harbor. The next day Dupont transferred his flag to the Ironsides, and the fleet, taking the flood-tide, passed safely over the bar, and came to anchor inside. The wooden vessels lay outside as a reserve. But just as everything was ready, a thick haze settled down over the water, obscuring the range, so that the attack had to be postponed.

As the eye swept around that bristling harbor, it was cannon here, and there, and everywhere. In front, lay Sullivan's Island to the right, and Morris Island on the left, the two points curving in towards each other till they approached within a mile. Midway in the channel, betwen them, built on an artificial island, stood Fort Sumter. Fort Moultrie, on Sullivan's Island, was opposite Sumter, while, above and below, batteries were erected on every available point. On the left, opposite this central fortress, stood battery Bee, on Cummings-Point, while beyond, should the vessels ever get there, battery succeeded battery, clear up to the city, three mile distant. Stretching down towards the fleet were other batteries on Morris Island, and among them Fort Wagner. The sight was enough to daunt the stoutest heart, for uncounted cannon lay shotted and aimed, ready to open on that little fleet. It was Dupont's purpose to pass as quickly as possible up the channel, and get to the west and northwest of Fort Sumter, which was known to be less impregnable than the front face.

At noon, the signal from the flag-ship to move to the attack was seen, and the little fleet, looking like mere rafts on the water, steamed slowly forward.

It was four miles to Fort Sumter, and the batteries of Morris Island commanded the whole distance. The vessels had advanced but a short distance before the Weehawken, leading the way with the strange machine in front, stopped, having got tangled up with the unweildy, novel thing. It took an hour to free herself, and then the fleet moved again. The fleet kept steadly on till opposite Fort Wagner, where they expected to meet the first blow of the hurricane; but all its guns kept motionless and still in their places, and only curious eyes greeted the advancing vessels. Next they floated by Battery Bee, but silence like death reigned over the low works. What does all this mean? This silence is ominous, and shows a confidence in something yet to come that portends no good. Still the fleet kept on; but just as the Weehawken was rounding-to to make the entrance of the harbor she came within the circle of fire from Forts Sumter and Moultrie. Then the crater opened from the top of Sumter, and down came a storm of shot and shell. Moultrie joined in, and thunder answered thunder with awful rapidity. The heavy metal fell like hailstones on the Weehawken; but she kept steadly on towards her assigned position, followed by the whole fleet. But suddenly she stopped in the very vortex of the fire. She had run upon a hawser stretched from Sumter to Moultrie, buoyed up on casks, and strung with nets, cables, and topedoes. Her propeller, getting entangled in these, became unmanageable, and she drifted helpless through the wild hurricane. The other vessels, as they came up, see the danger, and sheer off to try the channel on the other side of the fort. But here a row of piles is encountered, rising ten feet out of the water—while further up, the channel is crossed and recrossed with obstructions, backed by three iron-clads, that can hold those vessels under a fire that nothing that ever floated could survive. To add to the perplexity, the Ironsides, in the heavy tide, suddenly refused to obey her rudder, and she drifted towards Fort Moultrie, getting foul of the Catskill and Nantucket in her passage. The plan of the battle was now irrecoverably gone, and Dupont signalled to the fleet to disregard his movements. It was therefore every one for himself; and then was to be seen what splendid commanders Dupont had to second him in this unprecedented struggle. The gallant Rhind, left to act as he pleased, lays the Keokuk boldly alongside of the fort as though it were a ship, and with his little moniter makes a broadside engagement of it. Close behind him comes Rodgers in the Catskill, and, following hard after, the heroic Worden in the Montauk. A little further off lie the other vessels, all seeking to sound the full terrors of this awful abyss of fire. The gunners, stripped to their waists, and begrimed with powder and smoke, work their monster guns with a coolness and rappidity that tells fearfully on the solid face of Sumter.

Shot weighing four hundred and twenty pounds strike like heaven's own thunderbolts the trembling structure, but they are nothing to the answering shots that fall faster than the forge's hammer on their sides. Nothing built with mortal hands could long live there, and in thirty minutes the Keokuk came limping out fast settling in the waters. She had only been able to fire three times during the short period he was exposed to the guns of the enemy, and was obliged to withdraw from the action to prevent his vessel from sinking, which event occurred the following morning.

So unequal was the contest, which lasted less than forty minutes, that the entire fleet of iron-clads fired only one hundred and thirty-nine shots, though, during that same period, the enemy poured upon us an incessant storm of round-shot and shell, and rifle projectiles of all descriptions, and and red-hot shot.

The whole affair was so palpable and complete a failure, that the Department dared not directly blame Dupont for not succeeding. Still, reluctant to acknowledge itself any way in fault, it reproached him for not saying beforehand, how impossible success was. The simple truth is, the Secretary of the Navy, as well as the public generally, had come to have such a high opinion of the invulnerability of the iron-clads, that they considered Charleston as virtually ours, the moment the attack commenced. But, instead of complete success, this iron-clad fleet, the first ever set afloat and tested, effected absolutely nothing. It was too mortifying to confess the fact, without puting the blame on some one, and so it was placed on the commander, Dupont. He felt this keenly, and indignantly denounced the injustice of it.

In June Dupont was relieved from his command, and Admiral Foote ordered to take his place. The latter, however, was taken sick in New York, just as he was about to leave for his destination, and died.

The sudden death of Admiral Foote compelled the Department to reverse its order of removal, and to direct Dupont to resume his command.

July 6th, The Augusta left Port Royal, for Phila. with Admiral Dupont on board, made the passage in five days, nothing of interst occurring with the exception of "Splicing the Main-Brace" for the last time in the U. S. Navy, having been abolished by an act of Congress, through the influence of a few Down East Fanatics aided by Admiral Foote. On arriving at New-Castle, Del., the home of Dupont, we saluted and lowered his flag for ever.

Dupont was a superb man physically; of grand and imposing presence he trod the deck of his battle-ship like one of nature's noblemen. Even those accustomed to see men of distinguished personal appearance in various parts of the world, were stuck with the majesty and grandeur of his mien.

A gentleman of the old scheol, or rather a night of the olden time, his bearing was that of dignified courtesy to all, and impressed every one that approached him with profound respect. Chivalrous in his own feelings, he he was incapable of wounding those of others, while he was keenly sensitive to any censure upon his conduct. Insensible to fear, he never shrunk from encountering any danger, while he was too lofty and noble to rush into it to obtain mere notoriety. Master of his profession, he knew his duty better than the department that censured him, and experienced his greatest humiliation and suffering in performing it. Proud as he was sensitive, he could not brook unmerited rebuke. Irritated at his manly independence, the Government lost one of its best officers by gratifying its spleen, and under the pretence of maintaining its dignity. Dupont's name however will live long after those who persecuted him are consigned to forgetfulness, or to an immortality worse than oblivion.

The Augusta proceeded up the Del. to Phila. and on arriving there, found that great excitement prevailed all through the Northern States, in consequence of threatned invasion of Pennsylvania, by Gen. R. E. Lee, and rebel Privateers were making sad havoc among the Fishermen and Pilot boats along the coast. The Augusta took in a supply coal and went out in search of the pirates. After an unsuccessful cruise along the eastern coast, we retuned to New York, where the ship was put out of commisston, and the crew got leave of absence for Ten days. This ended the cruise of the U. S. S. Augusta.

DESCRIPTION

AND

CRUISE

OF THE

U. S. S. "Metacomet,"

WESTERN GULF BLOCKADING SQUADRON.

JAMES E. JOUETT,

Commander.

HENRY J. SLEEPER,

Lieut. & Ex. Officer.

The "Metacomet" was put in Commission at the Brooklyn Navy Yard January 4th, 1864, Captain James E. Jouett, Commanding, Henry J. Sleeper, Lieut. & Ex Officer. Was a double-ender, side-wheel, and was built expressly for river service. She was fitted with very powerful engines, and was considered to be the fastest vessel of her class in the service. Carried a battery of six IX inch broadside, one hundred pound Parrott rifle, and four Brass Howitzers.

Captain Jouett, had previously commanded the R. R. Cuyler, and had his crew detained on board the Receiving ship, until the Metacomet was ready for sea, he was heard to remark that, "he was going to do some fighting, and wanted a well-drilled ships' company." On Jan. the 4, the crew was transferred on board, and by request I was permitted to be one of their number. Immediately after going on board, nearly all the crew got forty-eight hours liberty, returned on time, and left the Navy Yard on the 26th, steamed down to Sandy Hook to adjust our compass, and left next morning for Key West. Had beautiful weather nearly all the passage. On Feb. the 5th, at five o'clock in the morning when off Abico, in a thick fog, run into the U. S. gun-boat Tioga, carrying away the the greater part of her wheelhouse and otherwise injured her, that we had to take her in tow. At six o'clock P. M. repaired some slight damages, and proceeded on our way to Key West, where we arrived Feb. 6th, took in a supply of coal, and left for New Orleans. Experienced very heavy weather on the passage. On the night of the 17th, carried away the fore Topmast, it was held aloft by the rigging and the ship rolling heavly, swung athwartships, taking full charge of both sides of the deck. The boatswain's mate passed the word, "lay forward the watch and clear away the wreck," no one responded to his call, and no one would venture forward, he immediately reported this to the Captain, who was on deck at the time. He procured a lantern and was in the act of going aloft himself, when he was met in the rigging by the writer, who had already been aloft, aud let the fragment of topmast down on deck, when he growled something about me being a Landsman, and had no business going aloft without orders. All this time the storm was increasing, shipping heavy seas forward which ripped up some of the planks in the forward part of the deck, and carried away part of the wheelhouse. On the morning of the 20th, the gale had abated, and the sea quite calm, went to work to send down the remainder of the broken topmast. Arrived at South-west Pass on the 21st, and anchored off the city of New Orleans in the afternoon, the ship was hauled alongside the "Levee" to undergo some repairs.

The boys being close to shore got restless, and when night came a great many of them improved their opportunity and took "French," some of them returned in a few hours, and the others determined to remain ashore all night but unfortunately eight of them fell into the hands of the Police and locked up for the night. Next morning Three of them were taken on board, the ship in the meantime, having hauled out into the stream, the boys upset the boat and gave them a ducking in the river, and came nearly drowning one of the policemen. On coming on board they demanded fifty dollars each for their prisoners. Capt. Jouett however, thought twenty-five dollars would pay them very well for their bath, which was accordingly paid them.

Left New Orleans, March 2nd, for the blockade off Mobile, where we remained without anything of interst occurring until the 7th. Our picket stationed in Swash Channel, discovered a steamer coming out, they kept quiet until she passed, and then fired a rocket in the direction she was going. The blockade runner saw our boat and went right out through the fleet, going so close to the "Oneida" that they could throw a biscuit on board. The "Richmond" fired four shots at her with what effect is not known. Three of the gun-boats chased her outside without success.

March 20th, the little steamer Cowslip, created quite a commotion by reporting the rebel ram Tennessee, coming out to attack the fleet. Everything was put in readiness to recieve her. The fleet formed in line of battle. and some of us thought we were going to attack the forts. About seven o'clock this idea was dispelled, and we were ordered to our anchorage

April 7th, at half-past two o'clock in the morning, our picket-b at, discovered a large steamer coming in, about four miles from our vessel, we signalized to her, and pulled alongside, and in ten minutes the boat was hoist, and then the chase commenced. The stranger had now turned, and was standing out to sea. It was now breaking daylight, and we lost sight of her, this did not last long, in a short time we got sight of her again, and headed for her. The Metacomet was now going through the water at a splendid rate. Capt. Jouett, sings out to the Engineer, to "Shake her up," and by six o'clock had her in range of our guns. We commenced firing at her with a 12 pound Howitzer, but she paid no attention to us whatever. We then tried another remedy, kept the ship off a couple of points and fired 100 pound rifle, this had the desired effect. They hauled down the English flag they had run up at daylight, and came around. They then kept on running towards us, (as they afterwards confessed) with the intention of running us down. Capt. Jouett saw this movement, and put a stop to it, by having a IX inch shell fired at them, which had the tendency of bringing them to a full stop. We immediately lowered our boats and went on board and took possession of her, and transferred all her crew on board our ship. The name of our prize was the "Donegal," from Havana. From some of her crew we were informed that the steamer "Denby," another blockade runner was coming in the following night. As usual at dusk, the Metacomet took her station in close to the beach, sending out a picket boat about two miles to the eastward, and there waited the coming of the "Denby." About two o'clock A. M. she made her appearance coming at full speed, directly for the picket boat, the rocket was fired, which was the signal to all the fleet. The Denby getting sight of our vessel altered her course and went for the ship channel. By this time all the fleet was underweigh. The night being very dark we could not tell friend from foe. By running up a light to the masthead, she got inside before it was discovered that she carried a white light instead of a red one, and by this Ruse she escaped being captured.

June the 29th, the steamer Glascow run a steamer ashore while trying to run the blockade. Next morning the gun-boats Pembina, Gennessee, and the sloop-of-war Monongahela, were sent in to destroy her. The shelled her until seven o'clock without much success. The Pembina came out, and the Metacomet took her place. We steamed in close to the beach, suddenly the rebels opened fire on us from a battery they had erected a few days previous. We returned the fire so rapidly that in half an hour their firing ceased. We then fired a few shell at the steamer, and came out to breakfast. After breakfast we went in again and commenced shelling the steamer, thinking the battery silenced, we went in closer to the beach, when the battery again opened on us, their first shell bursting over our wheel-house, one of the pieces coming in through the port, tearing a piece of the shirt-collar of a man in the act of sighting a gun, going through the right side and coming out on the left of another man standing in his rear. He died in six hours afterwards. Fort Morgan, who had been silent all the morning, now opened on us, sending shot and shell all around us, one of which passed through the forcastle. We then came out to let our guns cool, and then went in again, this time going right up to the battery, and consentrated all our fire on it, and in less than an hour it was silent, and remained so for that day. Next morning at daylight, we went about twenty miles out to sea for the purpose of burying the remains of Humphrey Fisher, who had been killed the day previous. When this ceremony was over, we returned to the fleet, and in a few minutes went in again and commenced shelling the steamer. The rebels then opened on us from Fort Morgan, and two other batteries, which we had not seen before, making it a little too hot for us, so we got out a little and commenced playing "long tom." On the morning of July the 4th, drew all the shot out of the guns, for the purpose of firing a National Salute. In the evening went in again to shell the batteries.

Next day was spent in making preparations for a boat expedition to burn the steamer. Everything arrainged, the boats came alongside at six o'clock. Three boats from the Hartford, in charge of Lieut. Watson, and one from the Brooklyn, the whole in command of our Capt. J. E. Jouett. About ten o'clock we started in towards the steamer, and sent a boat to reconnoiter. In about half an hour the boat returned and reported everything clear. The boats then pulled alongside the steamer and boarded her, spreading the turpen tine around the deck, and placing the powder under the Machinery set fire to her and jumped into the boats. We had hardly got on board when the rebels opened on us from the beach. This was the time which tested the courage of some of the young officers that accompanied this expedition. The Metacomet anchored under the guns of Fort Morgan, in order to cover the boats. As soon as the match was put to the turpentine, it illuminated the whole bay, the glistening baynots of the sentinels on Fort Morgan, was plainly visible, and the line of batteries on the beach, expecting every moment to be blown out the water. This was more than those young gentle-men could stand, and one of them forgot himself so far as to tell Capt. Jouett, that he ought to back out. One of the boats had not returned, and Capt. Jouett said he would not move an inch until every boat was alongside and every man safe on board. I dont think that any of those brave young gentlemen will ever care to accompany Capt. Jouett, on any more expedit-ions of this sort. The object of the expedition was to destroy the Machinery, so that it could not replace the old and worn out Machinery of some of the gun-boats inside the fort.

In the meantime, Farragutt arrived and made a reconnoissance of the forts and batteries, and vessels commanding the entrance to Mobile, for the purpose of obtaining an accurate knowledge of their strength. Morgan and Gaines were the chief forts barring it, and he gives the following as the results of his investigations:

FARRAGUT'S REPORT TO NAVY DEPARTMENT.

On the morning of the 20th I made a reconnoissance of Forts Morgan and Gaines. The day was uncommonly fine and the air very clear. We were distant from the forts three (3) miles, and could see everything distinctly, so that it was easy to verify the statement of the refugee McIntosh, in respect to the number of guns visible on the bastions of the fort. I could count the guns and the men that stood by them; could see the piles that had been driven across from Fort Gaines to the channel opposite Fort Morgan—the object of which is to force the ships to keep as close as possible to the latter. I am satisfied that if I had one iron-clad at this time, I could destroy their whole force in the bay, and reduce the forts at my leisure, by cooper ation with our land forces—say five thousand men. We must have about two thousand and five hundred men in the rear of each fort, to make regular approaches by land, and to prevent the garrison's receiving supplies and reinforcements; the fleet to run the batteries, and fight the flotilla in the bay. But without iron-clads, we should not be able to fight the enemy's vessels of that class with much prospects of success, as the latter would lie on the flats where our ships could not go and destroy them. Wooden vessels can do nothing with them unless by getting within one or two hundred yards, so as to ram them or pour in a broadside.

A month later he says:

I fully understand and appreciate my situation. The experience I had of the fight between the Arkansas and Admiral Davis's vessels on the Mississippi, showed plainly how unequal the contest is between iron-clads and wooden vessels in loss of life, unless you succeed in destroying the iron-clad. I therefore deeply regret that the Department has not been able to give us ONE of the many iron-clads that are off Charleston and on the Mississippi. I have always looked for the latter. but it appears that it takes us twice as long to build an iron-clad as any one else. It looks as if the con-tractors and the fates were against us. While the rebels are bending their whole energies to the war, our people are expecting the war to close by de-fault, and if they do not awaken to a sense of their danger soon, it will beso.

But be assured, sir, that the Navy will do its duty, let the issue come when it may, or I am greatly deceived,

A few weeks subsequent to this he says:

I ran in shore yeseerday, and took a good look at the iron-clad Tennessee. She flies the blue flag of Admiral Bnchanan. She has four ports of a side, out of which she fights, I undsrstand from the refugees, four 7-inch Brooks rifles, and two 19-inch columbiads. She has a torpedo flixture on the bow. Their four iron-clads and three wooden gun-boats made quite a formidable appearance.

Thus the winter and spring wore away, and mid-summer came before the preparations were completed for the contemplated attack. Farragut was at length informed that the iron-clad Tecumseh had arrived at Pensacola. there she was detained for want of coal, and had it not been for Captain Jenkins, of the Richmond, Craven said on his arrival, "God knows when I should have got here." He worked incessantly to carry out Farragut's wishes and the latter said of him, "He carries out the spirit of one of Lord Colling-wood's best sayings. 'Not to be afraid' of doing too much; those who are, seldom do as much as they ought.'"

July 19th, The Metacomet left the blockade, for New Orleans, for the purpose of convoying two Monitors from that port to Mobile. Crossed the bar at the mouth of the river at 6 30 A. M. and arrived at the foot of Canal street at 3 o'clock P. M. This was considered quick time against a five or six knot current.

On the 29th, left New Orleans for Mobile, acting as consort to the iron-clad Chickasaw. Arrived at the blockade on the 31st, and was immediatley ordered to Ship Island, for the monitor Winnebago, which had been towed there by the Tennessee.

In the meantime Farragut issued the following General Order:

FARRAGUT'S GENERAL ORDER.

"Strip your vessels and prepare for the conflict. Send down all your superfluous spars and rigging. Trice up or remove the whiskers. Put up the splinter-nets on the starboard side, and barricade the wheel and steers-men with sails and hammocks. Lay chains or sand-bags on the decks over the Machinery, to resist a plunging fire, Hang the sheet-chains over the side, or make any other arrangements for security that your ingenuity may suggest. Land your starboard boats, or lower and tow them to the port side, and lower the port boats down to the water's edge. Place a leadsman and the pilot in the port-quarter boat, or the one most convenient to the commander.

The vessels will run past the forts in couples, lashed side by side, as hereinafter designated. The flag-ship will lead, and steer from Sand Island N. by E. by compass, until abreast of Fort Morgan; then N. W. half N. until past the Middle Ground; then N. by W.; and the others, as designated in the drawing, will follow in due order, until ordered to anchor; but the bow and quarter line must be preserved, to give the chase-guns a fair range; and each vessel must be kept astern of the broadside of the next ahead. Each vessel will be kept a very little on the starboard quarter of his next ahead, and when abreast of the fort will keep directly astern, and as we pass the fort will take the same distance on the port-quarter of the next ahead, to enable the stern guns to fire clear of the next vessel astern.

It will be the object of the Admiral to get as close to the fort as possible before opening fire; the ships, however, will open fire the moment the enemy opens upon us, with their chase and other guns, as fast as they can be brought to bear. Use short fuses for the shell and shrapnel, and as soon as within three or four hundred yards, give the grape. It is understood that heretofore we have fired too high; but with grape-shot it is necessary to elevate a little above the object, as grape will dribble from the muzzle of the gun. If one or more of the vessels be disabled, their partners must carry them through, if possible; but if they cannot, then the next astern must render the required assistance; but as the Admiral contemplates moving with the flood-tide it will only require sufficent power to keep the crippled vessels in the channel.

Vesels that can, must place guns upon the poop and topgallant fore-castle, and in the tops on the starboard side. Should the enemy fire grape, they will remove the men from the topgallant forecastle and poop to the guns below, out of grape range. The howitzers must keep up a constant fire from the time they can reach with shrapnell until out of its range.

D. G. FARRAUT,
Rear Admiral, Commanding W. G. B. Squadron."

On the morning of August 2, we left the blockade for Pensacola, where we took on board a number of sand-bags, for the purpose of puting around the machinery, and making other neccessary preparations for passing the forts.

Left Pensacola at Ten o'clock on the morning of the 4th, in company with the steamer Bienville and monitor Tecumseh. Little did the crew of the Tecumseh think that this was their last day on earth. Some of them having expressed their sympathy for us, in having to pass the forts in a wooden gun-boat, while they considered themselves perfectly safe being in an iron-clad vessel.

We arrived at the blockade at 5 o'clock, and anchored for the night. Our orders were to get breakfast at 3 o'clock next morning, as this was the day we were to pass the forts, or perish in the attempt.

At daylight we were up and lashed to the gal'ant old Hartford. At half past six o'clock the advance commenced, the iron-clads taking the lead. When they had taken their positions, the wooden ships advanced in the following order linked as couples would enter a ball-room:

The Brooklyn, and Octorora, Hartford, and Metacomet, Richmond, and Port Royal, Lackawana, and Seminole, Monongahela, and Kennebec, Ossipee and Itasca, Oneida, and Galena, and the Admiral's steam barge "Loyal."

It was a novel position for Farragut to find himself in—following instead of leading—and one which he took very reluctantly, and only at the earnest solicitations of the officers, who said that the Brooklyn, having four chase guns to the Hartford's one, and also an ingenious machine for picking up torpedoes, with which they knew the channel to be lined, should be the leading vessel. They stated, moreover, that in their judgment the flag-ship, on the movements and signals of which all the other movements depended, should not be so much exposed as she would be at the head of the line, for she might be crippled before they came up with the forts. Farragut demurred very much to this arrangement, saying that "exposure was one of the penalties of rank in the navy;" besides, it did not matter where the flag-ship was, "she would always be the main target for the enemy."

The fleet, with the Brooklyn ahead, steamed slowly on, and at a quarter to seven the Tecumseh fired the first gun. About twenty minutes later the forts and water batteries opened a murderous fire. When about five hundred yards from Fort Morgan the Brooklyn grounded slightly and begin to back, causing the order to reverse engines to pass down through the whole fleet, and bringing it to a sudden halt, just as it was entering the fiery vortex. " What could this mean," had hardly leaped to the lips of Farragut, when he heard the cry, "The Metacomet is on fire!" "The Tecumseh is going down!" Glancing his eye to the spot where she lay, he saw only the top of her turrets rapidly disapearing beneath the water. The sight at this moment was enough to try the stoutest heart, and it brought out, like a flash of lightning, all the heroism in the man. What! his whole line halted— The Tecumseh, for which he had waited so long, as the only match in the fleet for the ram Tennessee, gone to the bottom with all her noble crew, and the fiery tempest full upon him! With his usually mild face now blazing with the light of battle, and unalterable resolution written on every line-ment, he shouted out, in a voice that rung over the thunder of cannon, " Go ahead!" and both ships dashed to the head of the line, and hoisted the signal " close action," we drove straight for the blazing fort, followed by the squadron.

A boat was lowered from our ship and manned, in charge of a gallant and courageous young officer named Neil, and went to the rescue of the few who were fortunate enough to escape from the turret of the Tecumseh. It was a grand sight to behold that little boat pulled towards the strugling forms in the water, with the Stars and Stripes flying to the breese, amidst the shower of shot and shell that was falling around them as thick as hail from both friends and enemies. They succeeded in saving ten of them, four were seen to swim ashore to the fort.

All this time the battle continued, the Hartford and Metacomet, having the lead. The rebel fleet were drawn up in line to dispute our entrance into the bay, and was raking us fore and aft. We could not return the fire only with one gun from the Hartford. A shell from the ram Tennessee, struck us forward, and entered the store-room and exploded close to the magazine. Our situation looked critical. Captain Jouett, seeing how we were situated, several times asked the Admiral who was still in the rigging, to let us go. To this Farragut would not consent, until he was out of range of the forts.

The author, from his position at the forward pivot gun, was directly under the main-rigging of the Hartford, where Farragut was lashed, and could hear almost every order he give. He was not lashed with a hammock-lashing, nor yet a yarn whipped over one of the shrouds, as some of our historians describes him. The facts are those; he secured himself in the port main-rigging, with a piece of rattling-stuff, so as to prevent his falling between the two ships, and, was not so close to the top as to put his hand up through the lubber's hole, and seize the foot of his pilot Martin Freeman, and besides he would not be able to watch the movements of the fleet in this position. When we got past the fort, Farragut give the order to let go! there was no time to be lost in casting the hawser adrift that held us to the Hartford, taking the battle-axe from my belt, with a few blows cut the lines, and went flying past the Hartford up the bay in pursuit of the rebel gun-boats who started to run when they seen us pass the forts. The chase did not last long, in about twenty minutes we had them in range. Then the action commenced in earnest. The Morgan, and Gaines, were on our starbord side, and the Selma, on our port. This cross-fire did not last long, after pouring a few broadsides into the Gains, she made for the beach in a sinking condition. The Morgan soon followed running under the guns of Fort Morgan. Those two obstacles removed, we turned all our guns on the Selma, and a few minutes the shell, grape and canister, were going over and into her, at a fearful rate, causing a great loss of life. In about half an hour she struck her colors in token of surrender. We immediately sent a boat on board, when they got there a horrible sight met the eye. The dead and dying were heaped up together, and mangled forms lay everywhere to be seen. Their loss in this engagement which lasted only thirty minutes, was twenty-nine killed, and fifteen wounded. Among the former were Lieut. Comstock, who was in the act of sighting a gun, when he was hit, and his remains were found lying over the breach of the gun. And among the latter Captain Murphy, severely in the neck and arm, Notwithstanding that Capt. Murphy was a rebel officer, he deserves great credit, for the manner in which he fought his ship, and had the other rebel commanders followed his example, they would have made it pretty hot for us. Capt. Murphy had formerly been U. S. officer, and is another evidence to show what brave men our navy had been formerly composed of. When our men went on board to hoist the flag, they found the halyards were unrove, this did not detain them long, in a minute one of them climbed up the flag staff and with a strip of his handkerchief made the Stars and Stipes fast, where the rebel flag had been flying a few minutes before.

The other vessels following in the wake of the flag-ship, one after another swept past the batteries, the crews cheering loudly, and were signal-led by the flag-ship to come to anchor. But they had scarcely commenced clearing up the decks when the rebel ram was seen boldly standing out into the bay, and steering straight for the fleet, with the purpose of attacking it. The moment Farragut discovered it, he signalled the vessels to run her down, and, hoisting up his own anchor, ordered the pilot to drive the Hartford full on the monster. The Monongahela, under the command of the intrepid Strong, being near the rear of the line, was still moving up the bay when he saw the ram heading for the line. He instantly sheered out, and ordering a full head of steam, drove with tremendous force straight on the iron-clad structure. He struck her fair, then, swinging round, poured a broadside of eleven-inch shot, which, fired at such close range, fell with the weight of descending rocks on her mailed side. Yet they bounded back, and dropped harmlessly into the water. Wheeling, he again stuck her, though he had carried away his own iron prow and cutwater. The Lackawana came next, and stricking the ram while under full headway, rolled her over on her side. Such was the force of the shock that her own .stern was cut and crushed to the planks for a distance of three feet above the water's edge to five feet below, springing her aleak. If his yards and topmasts had not been down, they would have gone overboard under the shock. As the vessel swung around broadside to, a gunner succeeded in planting a nine-inch shell, fired within twelve feet of the ram, into one of the shutters, breaking it in to fragment, which were driven into the case-uate. The rebels could be seen through the portholes making defiant gest-ures, while the cursed and blackguarded our crew in revolting language, which so exasperated them that they fired on them with muskets, and even hurled a spitoon and holy-stone at them, which made them scatter. The next moment, down came Farragut in the Hartford, but just before the vessel struck, the ram sheered so that the blow was a glancing one, and the former rasped along her iron-plated hull and fell alongside. Recoiling for some ten or twelve feet, the Hartford poured in at that short distance a whole broadside of nine-inch solid shot, hurled with charges thirteen pounds of powder. The heavy metal, though sent with such awful force, and in such close proximity, made no impression, but broke into fragments on the mailed sides, or dropped back into the water. The shot and shell from the Tennessee, on the other hand, went crushing through and through the wooden sides of the hartford, strewing her deck with the dead. One 150-pound shell, exploding inside, prostrated men on the right hand and left, one of the fragments going through the spar and berth decks, and clean through the launch into the hold among the wounded.

The Hartford now stood off, and began to make a circuit in order to come down again, when the Lackawana, which was driving the second time on the monster, struck by accident the Hartford a little forward of the mizzen mast, and cut her down to within two feet of the water. She was at first thought to be sinking, and "the Admiral! the Admiral!—save the Admiral!" rang all over the ship. But Farragut, seeing that the vessel would still float, shouted out to put on steam, determined to send her, crushed and broken as she was, full on the ram.

By this time the monitors had crawled up, and were pouring in their heavy shot. The Chickesaw got under the stern and knocked away the smokestack, while the Manhattan sent one shot clean through the vessel, and disabled her stern port shutter with a shell, so that the gun could not be used, while a third carried away the steering gear. Thus, with her steering-chains gone, her smokestack 'shot away, many of her port shutters jammed, the Tennessee stood at bay among the hounds, while the Ossipee, Le Roy commanding, was now driving towards her under full headway; and a little farther off, bearing down on the same awful errand, were coming the Hartford, Monongahela and Lackawana. The fate of the poor vessel was now sealed, and her commander hoisted the white flag, but not until the Ossipee was so near, that Le Roy could not prevent a collision, and his vessel rasped heavily along the iron sides of the ram. He received her surrender from commander Johnson—the Admiral, Buchanan, having been previously wounded in the leg. This ended the morning's work, and, at ten minutes past ten, the fleet came to anchor within four miles of Fort Morgan.

The killed and wounded on board the fleet amounted to two hundred and twenty-two—among the latter was Captain Mallory, of the Galena. Fifty-two were killed, of which twenty-five, or about half, were killed on board the Hartford, showing to what a fearful fire the flag-ship had been exposed, The Brooklyn was the next severest sufferer, receiving the heaviest fire of the fort.

The loss of the Tecumseh, with her gallant commander Craven and his crew, nearly all of whom went to the bottom, chastened somewhat the joy over this great victory. Craven was in the turret when the torpedo exploded, which almost lifted the iron-clad from the water, and blowing such a huge opening in her bottom that she sunk before the men from below could go on deck.

The only other vessel lost was the Phillipi, which followed the fleet against orders, and being struck by a shot was run ashore by her commander and deserted, when the rebels burned her.

Some idea of the terrible fire that had rolled over the waters that morning may be obtained by reflecting what an enormous amount of powder must have been exploded, since the Hartford and Brooklyn alone fired nearly five thousand pounds. The fleet and batteries together must have expended enough if put together, to have lifted the city of Mobile bodily from its foundations.

Two days after the victory, Farragut issued the following order:

FLAG-SHIP HARTFORD,

Mobile Bay, August 7th, 1864.

The Admiral desires the fleet to return thanks to the Almighty God for the signal victory over the enemy on the morning of the 5th instant.

D. G. FARRAGUT,

Rear-Admiral Commanding W. G. B. Squadron.

The night after the battle, Fort Powel was evacuated, the rebels blowing it up. The next morning the Chickesaw went down and shelled Fort Gains, and the following morning Colonel Anderson, the commander, sent a note to Farragut, offering to surrender, and asking for terms. The reply was, first, unconditional surrender. When this was done the prisoners should be treated in conformity with the custom of civilized nations, and private property, with the exception of arms, be respected. These terms were accepted, and at a quarter to ten o'clock the same morning the rebel flag came down, and the stars and stripes went up, amid the loud and prolonged cheers of the fleet.

Fort Morgan still refused to surrender, and Gen. Granger having perfected his seige operations, the fleet moved down on Sunday night, the 21st, and next morning at daybreak opened a terrific bombardment upon it. The batteries on shore joined in with their overwhelming fire, and all day long it rained a horrible tempest on the devoted fort Farragut said: "A more magnificent fire has rarely been kept up." The inhabitants of Mobile gathered on the shores and house-tops and towers to gaze on the terrific scene, while the buildings, though miles away, rattled under the awful explosions, and one vast sulphurous cloud heaved and tossed above the quiet waters of the bay. Just at twilight the citadel of the fort took fire, and the garrison, finding themselves unable to extinguish the flames, which now shot heavenward in the increasing darkness, flooded the magazine to prevent its blowing up, and threw large quantities of powder into the wells.

All night long the bombardment was kept up, ribbing the darkness with ghastly seams of light, as shells crossed and recrossed each other in their fiery track.

Thus the fearful night wore on, and at six in the morning a dull heavy explosion came over the bay from the smoking fort, and half an hour latter a white flag was seen to wave from the ramparts. General Page offered to surrender the fort, and asked the terms. The same as those given to Fort Gaines were offered and accepted. In his impotent rage, however, the Commander ordered all the guns to be spiked, the carriages disabled, and arms, ammunition, &c., destroyed. He also, with some other officers, broke their swords, under the silly impression that this would lessen the humiliation of the surrender.

"The whole conduct of the officers of Fort Gaines and Fort Morgan," said Farragut, "presents such a striking contrast in moral principal that I cannot fail to remark upon it. Colonel Anderson, who commanded the former, finding himself in a position perfectly untenable, and encumbered with a superfluous number of conscripts, many of whom were mere boys, determined to surrender a fort which he could not defend, and in this determination was supported by all his officers save one; but, from the moment he hoisted the white flag, he scrupulously kept everything intact, and in that condition delivered it over; whilst General Page and his officers, with a childish spitefulness, destroyed the guns which they had said they would defend to the last, but which they never defended at all, and threw away or broke those weapons which they had not the manliness to use against their enemies; for Fort Morgan never fired a gun after the commencement of the bombardment, and the advanced pickets of our army were actually on its glacis."

As before stated, the ceremony of surrender took place at two P. M., and the same afternoon the garrison was sent to New Orleans in the United States steamer Tennessee and Bienville, where they arrived safely.

BLOWING UP THE RAM NASHVILLE.

On the evening of the 24th, a boat expedition left our ship in charge of Ex. officer Henery J. Sleeper, for the pupose of destroying the unfinished ram Nashville, which was partly sunk in the channel, just inside the fort at Dog river bar, to prevent our gun-boats from getting up to the city of Mobile. We left the ship at nine o'clock, taking everything that was necessary for the destruction of this formidable ram, which the rebels intended to use as a battery against us if we attempted to cross the bar. We pulled along-side cautiously and entered through the port-holes, spreading turpentine around the deck, and placing the powder and shell in a good position set her on fire and jumped into the boats. The officer in charge of the expedition after applying the match beat a hasty retreat through the port-hole, and in his excitement fell headlong into the boat on top of the writer who was holding on in the bow of the boat, and was compelled to throw him over my head into his boat on the outside of us before I could shove my boat off. We had only got a short distance from the ram when the powder exploded tearing her upper works all to pieces. Seeing a couple of river steamers coming in our direction, the boys gave way with a will and soon reached the ship in safety, then steamed down the bay to the fleet.

Thursday Aug. 25th, at one o'clock a boat from our ship, and one from the Seminole, left the flag-ship Hartford, for the purpose of putting a buoy on the spot where the ill-fated monitor Tecumseh went down on the morning of the 5th. We succeeded in doing this, and was returning to our ship when Martin Freeman Farragut's pilot, proposed that we should drag some of the torpedos from the channel. This proposition was accepted by the greater part of our men, we immediately went to work and in a short time had five of them on the beach. One of those were about to be removed by Mr. Freeman's orders and placed by itself when it exploded. I had just let go the rope and sat down in the sand for the purpose of taking off my shoes to go into the water after the others when the explosion took place. I was slightly stunned by the explosion and hardly knew what to do, I rushed around from one to the other with the intention of assisting my own comrades first. The groans of the wounded men were dreadful. They were mutilated past recognition. I came to one whom I recognized as the cockswain of my boat, he was so mangled that I could render him no assistance. Fort Morgan at this time was garrisoned by colored troops, some of which were lounging around the beach, was called upon to assist us in draging the torpedos out of the water, several of them took hold of the rope and was hauling away when the explosion occurred. One them was so close to the the torpedo that it blowed all his clothes completly off, he was lying with his face downward in the sand and hollering with all his might. When I came to him I rolled him over, and found that he had not received even a scratch, told him to get upon his feet that he was not hurt, and immediately saw him going in the direction of Fort Morgan roaring like a wild man. Next came to another which I recognized by a portion of his uniform which was still burning, as Acting Ensign White, in charge of our boat. He was badly burned about the face and body, I immediately clasped him in my arms and pressing his clothing close to mine, succeeded in extinguishing the fire. He asked my name and said "for God sake take me on board, and save my life." I mustered all my strength and carried him to the boat, and supported him in my arms while we were towed alongside the ship.

The Metacomet remained in Mobile bay until the city was taken, having several engagements with the batteries along the eastern shore, and had many narrow escapes from being blown up with torpedos.

This ended my cruise on the Metacomet, I was transferred to the flag-ship Hartford, and afterwards to the steamer Fort Morgan, to return to New York, where I was discharged from the U. S. Navy, October 10, 1864.

F. M'CARTEN,

DESCRIPTION

AND

Cruise of the U. S. Flag-ship

"Tennessee,"

Captain W. W. LOW,
AND
Captain JONATHAN YOUNG,   } COMMANDING.

Rear Admiral WILLIAM REYNOLDS,

AND

Rear Admiral THOMAS H. PATTERSON,

Commanding U. S. Naval Force on the Asiatic Station.

1878.

TENNESSEE'S "YOUNG AMERICA" PRESS.

The Tennessee (formerly the Madawaska,) was built at the Brooklyn Navy Yard in 1865, and was fitted out with Isherwood's patent engines. On her trial-trip in New York bay she made seventy-six (76) miles in four hours. In 1870 she made a trip to San Domingo with the Commissioners, and returned to New York in the same year, and was put out of commission, another deck was put on her, and received a pair of John Roache's back acting compound engines. She is a frigate-built clipper, with two fighting decks, berth-deck, cock-pits, poop-deck and top-gallant forecastle.

DIMENSIONS OF HULL.

Lenght between perpendiculars	.... 335 feet.
" Overall	.... 375 "
Breath of beam	45 ft. 2 in.
Depth of hold	31 "
Draft of watar when ready for sea (aft)	22 " 6 "
" " " " forward	20 " 3 "

PRINCIPAL SPARS.

Lenght of fore lower-mast	119 feet.
" main " "	123 " 4 in.
" mizzen " "	95 " 4½ "
" fore yard	87 "
" main "	97 "
" cro'jack	66 "
Height of fore royal truck above water line	185 "
" :" main " " " "	191 "
" " mizzen " " " '	154 "

BATTERY 23 GUNS.

18 IX inch on Main deck	Weight of shot	90 lbs.
2 XI inch pivots on Spar deck	"	166 "
2 100 pdr. Parrott "	"	70 "
1 60 pdr. Parrott on top-gallant forecastle.		60 "

She is provided with several Dahlgren howitzers for boat and field service, a battery of Gattling guns, small arms and pikes sufficient to arm all hands. She also carries torpedo out-riggers with permanent wires running fore and aft inside the bulwarks connecting with portable batteries on the quarter-deck by which four heavy torpedoes can be simultaneously exploded under the water line fifty feet from the ship's side; and has the necessary apparatus for using the " Harvey " torpedo.

CAPACITY OF MAGAZINES.

238—200 pound Tanks.
21—150 "   "
34—100 "   "
68—50   "   "

CAPACITY OF SHELL-ROOM

1170 IX inch shell
180 XI   "   "
190 100 pdr. "
95   60   "   "
100 12   "   "
54   12   " . " (light)
31   XI   inch shrapnel
180 IX   "   "
50   100 pdr.   "
25   60   "   "
10   12   "   "
162 "   "   " (light)

Capacity of provisions, four months for four hundred men.

Capacity of water tanks 7526 gallons.

Maximum quanity of water that can be distilled in twenty-four hours, 100 gallons per hour.

DESCRIPTION OF ENGINES.

Two back acting compound engines. Maximum indicated horse power 1640. Ten (10) Cylinderical boilers of two furnaces each. Grate surface 478 square feet.

CAPACITY OF COAL-BUNKERS.

380 Tons.

Coal consumed at full power 67 tons,   } Bituminous.
"   "   at ¾   "   50   "

CHAIN CABLES & ANCHORS.

Cables, 2 bower 165 fathoms, 2 sheet 150 fathoms, and 1 stream 105 fathoms.

Anchors.	2 bowers	7520	} Lbs.	2 sheet	8150·	} Lbs.
		7650			7350	
"	1 stream	2143	"			

SAIL AREA.

Total area		44, 289, 22	"	square feet.
Available at one time		39, 497, 07	"	" "
All plain sail	"	26, 807, 05	"	" "

Displacement   "   4220   "   "   square feet.

Tonnage   "   2135   "   "   tons.

CRUISE OF THE "TENNESSEE."

The Tennessee was put in commission at the Brooklyn navy yard May 1st, 1875. Her crew was transferred from the U. S. Recieving ship Vermont, May 20th She cast her moorings on dock off June 15th, and steamed down the river and anchored off the battery at five P. M.

June 15th, hoisted and saluted the Flag of Rear Admiral William Reynolds, U. S. N., Commanding U. S. Naval Force on the Asiatic Station.

"SALUTE TO THE FLAG"

Unfurl to the breese, on land and on Sea,
Our emblem of liberty, the Flag of the free,
The army shall weild it as their Septre of power,
The Navy shall sheild it as the hope of the hour,
While the South with the North proclaim in one Voice,
The flag of our Union is the flag of our choice.

June 26th, left our anchorage off the battery, and steamed down the bay, and came to anchor at Staten Island.

Out-ward Bound.

June 27th, at 10 A. M. left our anchorage Staten Island, passed Sandy Hook, discharged pilot and set our course for Gibraltar, distance 3180 miles.

July 4th, 1875.

July 4th, Sunday–At meridian hove ship too, and celebrated the 99th. anniversary of American Independence by firing a salute of 21 guns. Lat. 42 41' N, Long. 42, 07' W- distance from Gibraltar 1712 miles.

On the 13th, land reported at 4 A. M. coast of Spain plainly visible. At eight o'clock made out the coast of Africa. At 9 A. M. came to anchor off Gibraltar.

Gibraltar.

A rocky promontory, 3 miles in lenght, and 3-4 of a mile in average breath. and greatest elevation 1, 349 feet, near the southern extremity of Spain, at the entrance to the Mediterruean, everywhere fortified by works of great strength and extent, connected on the north by a low istmus with Andalusia, Five miles across the bay is the Spanish town of Algerias between which and Gibraltar lies the Bay of Gibraltar, also called the Bay of Algesiras, which is about eight miles long, by five broad, with a depth in the centre of upwards of 100 fathoms. The anchorage is not good, and the bay is much exposed, especially to the S. W. winds, which occasionally do great damage to the shipping. Gibraltar was taken in 1704 by a combined Dutch and English force, under Sir George Rooke, after a vigorous bombardment, and since that time it has remained continuously in possession of the British, notwithstanding the desperate efforts on the part of France and Spain to dislodge them. Gibraltar being a free port, is resorted to by Spanish smuglers, who drive a thriving trade by introducing contraband goods into Spain.-Total population in 1871 (including 6,521 military), 25,216.

Gibraltar is said to be the strongest fortified place in the world, it mounts a gun for every day in the year, consequently has at present 1875.

The officers of the Tennessee, gave a Ball in honor of the British officers of Gibraltar, and which was well attended by Citizens, Soldiers, and their wifes. Some of the soldiers acted in a very disorderly manner on leaving the ship.

Palermo, Sicily.

We made a very successful passage from Gibraltar to this port, in one hundred hours. Distance 1250 miles.

Palermo, is one of the most beautiful cities it has ever been my lot to visit. It is situated in a most lovely bay, which supplies splendid anchorage for vessels of all denominations, and whose calm blue waters, no rough, or stormy sea ever ruffles. The city itself is surrounded by a chain of lofty hills, and has a charming drive all round its walls, passing over a long and handsomely arched viaduct, which gives one the idea of an old Roman encampment. The inhabitants are polite and highly cultivated in the arts and sciences, Religion, Poetry, Painting and Sculpture, flourish here. The houses are of great architectural beauty. There are handsome streets and promenades, in and about the city, and every evening, during the summer months, a Band discourses realy fine music, to such as are willing to lend a listening ear. The Catacombs, or places of interment for the dead, here, will well repay a visit. Hewn out of the solid rock, and in places assisted by natural excavations, they present a singular and striking spectacle. Whole families in grim and ghastly skeleton array, are here, standing side by side, in those cavernous recesses, grouped in accordance with their age and sex whilst living, the maidens only being distinguished from the other members of the family by a small silver crown encircling their skulls, a monk acting as guide, shows you round. Interments in these vast catacombs take place every day with much pomp and ceremony in accordance with the rites of the Catholic church.

Then in the evenings the Grand Gardens, are a great resort, and as the shades of night draw nigh, you will see the fair Italian maidens and Nobility, taking their evening promenade. Next to the Ladies, the fruits are the handsomest products of the place, for a few cents only. I obtained a large handful of Peaches, Pears, and Grapes.

The Italian Soldiery, also struck me as being particularly sturdy and hardy looking, though lacking althogether, that air of discipline so necessary to well drilled Troops.

Palermo is the Capital of Sicily, was taken by General Garibaldi, in 1862. The Gen. make residence at this place, he was absent from the city during our stay at this port, consequently we were greatly disapcinted in not seeing the great "red shirt" warrior. Altogether Palermo is very beautiful and interesting place, would that I had more time to visit the interior.

The Tennessee enlarged her Band, by shipping a number of Italy's famous Musicians.

Left Palermo, August 8th, for Port Said, passed through the Straits of Messenia, sighted "Ætna" Sicily's famous burning mountain. The scenery is beautiful and picturesque. Passed Candiere Island, one of the Crecian Archepelago.

Aug. 12th, arrived at Port Said, this is the entrance to the canal. There is nothing of any importance to be seen, being nothing more than a coaling station for vessels going through the canal. It presents a desolate appearance, not a sign of vegetation to be seen, nothing but a vast sand desert as far as the eye can see. Population 3,500, chiefly Arabs, French, English and Jews. A number of Arabs came on board for the purpose of coaling ship, and engaged in a free-fight among themselves, we were compelled to put them ashore for the sake of peace. Those however, cannot be considered as a fare specimen of the race.

The Arab.

The Arab is of medium stature, muscular make, and brown complexion. Earnestness and lofty pride look out of his glowing eyes; by nature he is quick, sharp-witted, lively, and passionately fond of poetry. Courage, temperance, hospitality, and good faith, are his leading virtues; but these are often marred by a spirit of sanguinary revenge and rapacity. His wife keeps the house and educates the children. The Arab cannot conceive a higher felicity than the birth of a camel or a foal, or that his verses should be honored with the applause of his tribe.

The Suez Canal.

The Suez Canal–said to one of the wonders of the age, and in which the English Goverment has invested the sum of £ 4, 000 000 is attracting a large portion of the trafic between England and the East, and will probably compel her to take an active part in supporting the Khedive.

The canal is eighty-seven miles in lenght, vessels passing through are not allowed to steam faster than four miles an hour, thus it took the "Tennessee" two days to go through. The canal is very narrow, just wide enough for any size vessel to go through, with the exception of the stations or Gares, where the vessels pass each other. There are Telegraph stations situated all along the canal, and vessels entering are Telegraphed from one station to another, thus the Company can tell exactly where the vessels passing through are.

The first day going through, the land on both sides as far as the eye can see, is one wide expanse of white sand. The second, we pass now and then, through high land, and the soil is not quite so barren, at places a sparse vegetation had sprung up.

The Caravan and Camel.

Here you can see the Camel in his natural element, we saw several Caravans crossing the desert.

Caravan, the name given to the great assemblages of travelers which, at stated times, traverse the deserts of Asia and Africa. Many caravans are entirely for the purposes of trade, the merchants associating themselves for mutual help and protection. A Caravan sometimes has so many as 1000 camels, which follow each other in single file, so that it may be a mile or more in lenght. The most celebrated caravans are those formed by pilgrims going to Meca, particularly those which annually assemble at Cairo and at Damascus. The latter consists of 30 000 to 50,000 pilgrims, and is under the special protection of the Turkish sultan. The trade between Tripoli and the interior of Africa is exclusively carried on by caravans, also that between Darfur and Egypt.

Lake Ishmailia.

Aug. 14th, came to anchor off a beautiful village called Ishmalia in Lake Morah, which means " bitter water," a large white house can be seen among the trees on shore, it is said to be the Governor's house. Great clouds of sand are lifted from the desert, and carried across the plains, burying everything in its route. One of those storms can now be seen rising, passing over the little village, which completely obscure it from our view.

Suez City.

We passed out of the canal and came to anchor off Suez City. Ten miles from our anchorage is said to be the place where Moses led the Children through the Red Sea. It is also asserted by an old sailor on board this ship (Jacob Stoppernot), that he was on board a ship that once anchored near this place, and hoisted one of the wheels of " Pharoah's Chariot" on the fluke of her anchor. "Jacob has never been known to tell a lie."

Aug. 16th, Admiral Reynolds and wife, and a party of officers left the ship, for the purpose of visiting the Pyramids at Cairo, Egypt.

Colors of the Ocean.

The ocean has naturally a pure bluish tint. All profound and clear seas are all more or less of a deep blue; while, according to seamen, a green color indicates soundings. The bright blue of the Mediterranean, so often vaunted by poets, is found all over the deep, pure ocean, not only in the tropical and temperate zones, but also in the regions of eternal frost. The North Sea is green, partly from the reflection of its sandy bottom mixing with the essentially blue tint of the water. The pecular coloring of the red sea, whence its name, is derived from the presence of a microscopic algæ, or sea weed less remarkable even for its beautiful red color than for its prodigious fecundity. The evening after the Tennessee left Suez, a most remarkable color of water was noticed, the ship seemed to be sailing through an ocean of milk, a phenomenon which was owing to the immense number of little white animals swiming on the surface.

We made the passage across the Red Sea, in five days. Passed the Twelve Apostals (Islands), they are named after each of the Apostals.

Aden, Arabia.

Aug. 26th, arrived at Aden, a very important fortified town on a small peninsula of the south coast of Arabia, 118 miles from the entrance to the Red Sea, taken by Great Britain in 1839. The territory, is under the administration of the Goverment of Bombay, comprises an area of between 18 and 20 miles, and is of volcanic origin, consisting chiefly of a range of hills, which rise from 1.000 to 1.760 feet high. It enjoys almost perpetual sunshine, a cloudy day being very rare. It is a place of considerable strength, and, like all British possessions is well garrisoned, its situation between Asia and Africa, resembling that of Gibraltar, between Europe and Africa. Its excellent port render it a valuable station en route from India to Europe as a coaling depot. The population is nearly 30.000 including troops and followers.

The Tennessee, remained only two days at this port, just long enough to take in a supply of coal, and left for Bombay.

Bombay, India.

The Island of Bombay was part of the dowry of the Infanta of Portugal, and was made over by Charles the II. to the East India Company in 1668. The total area of this province is not far short of that of Germany, native States occupying about one-third; Sind, a non-regulation province, one-fourth; and Bombay proper, once the territory of the Peishwa, the remaining 82.000 square miles.

The length of the province is 1.050 miles and it has many fine natural harbors. Of the inhabitants 75 per cent are Hindoos, who worship Juggernaut—a God who used to be dragged through the streets in his Chariot, and the native would fall down and worship. So great was their infatuation, that the women would throw their children beneath the wheels of the Chariot to be crushed to death. Their idea seeming to be that, greater the torture on earth, the greater happiness they would experience in heaven. These heathen ideas however, was done away with by the English after the sacrifice of many lives. Bombay is yearly rising in importance as the great commercial port of India. After London it is the most populous city in the British Empire. During our week stay at this port the weather was constantly overcast and it rained incessantly.

Colombo.

We made the passage to this port in four days. It is an Island in the Indian Ocean, to the south-east of the peninsula of Hindustan, is situated in Latitude 70 40' N, long. 80 34' E. It has an area of 24, 702 square miles. Its greatest length from north to south, 266 square miles, and greatest width 140 miles. In 1505, the potuguese formed settlements on the island but were dispossed in the next century by the Dutch. In 1705, the British took possession of the Dutch settlements on the island, and annexed them to the Presidency of Madras; but six years after, 1801 it contained a population 2, 405, 287, of whom the most numerous were the Singhalese, descendants of colonists from the valley of the Ganges, who first settled in the island B. C. 543.

The Island is a rich and valuable one, the breeses blowing off the shore bring with them the sweet odor of spices, of which the island abounds.

Natural Scenery.

In natural scenery, Ceylon can vie with any part of the world; and as it rises from the ocean, clothed with the rich luxuriance of a tropical vegetation, it seems to the voyager like some enchanted island of Eastern story. Its hills, draped with forests of perennial green, tower grandly from height to height, till they are lost in clouds and mist. Near at hand, a sea of sapphire blue dashes against the battlemented rocks that occur at isolated points, and the yellow strands are shaded by groves of noble palms. In shape, Ceylon, resemble a pear, but its inhabitants more poetically compare it to one of their elongated pearls. Undulating plains cover about four parts of the island, and the fifth is occupied by the mountain-zone of the central south, which has an elevation of 8,000 feet above the level of the sea. Pedrotallagalla, the highest mountain in the range, attains the height of 8280 feet; the celebrated mountain of Adam's Peak is 7420 feet.

Manners and Customs.

The inhabitants in their customs, and costume, and general appearance, have remained unchanged since the days of ptolemy. The dress of the men, who have delicate features and slender limbs, is singularly effeminate, and consists of a COMBOY or waist-cloth, very much resembling a petticoat; their long hair, turned back trom the forehead, is confined with combs, and earings are worn by way of ornament. The women, in addition-to the

COMBOY, cover the upper part of the figure with a white muslin jacket, and adorn themselves with necklaces, bangles, rings, and jewellery. The Singh-alese are false and cowardly, but manifest a strong affection for their relatives, and a reverance for old age. Polyandry still lingers in the interior of Ceylon, and was formerly universal; it is now, however, chiefly confined to the wealthier classes, amongst whom one woman has often three or four husbands. The Kandyans, or Highlanders, are a more sturdy race, and maintained their independance for three centuries after the the conquest of the low country by European settlers. The Malabars, or Tamils, have sprung from those early invaders of Ceylon, who from time to time swept across from Southern Hindustan, and contended with the Singhalese kings for the sovereignty of the island.

The 'burghers' of Ceylon are a people of European descent, who have become naturalized. Those of Portuguese extraction hold the lowest place, but the Dutch burghers frequently fill responsible posts, and are employed in the goverment offices.

The Veddahs.

Besides the races already alluded to, there is a remarkable tribe of out casts—the Veddahs—hardly removed from the wild animals of the forest, and believed to be descended from the Yakkhos, the aboriginal inhabitants of the country. They occupy a district in the eastern part of the island, and have there preserved their ancient customs, and manner of living unaltered for more than 2000 years. They appear to be without the instinct of worship, and have no knowledge of a God. The tribe is divided into the Rock Veddahs and the village Veddahs. The former hide themselves in the jungle, live by the chase, and sleep in trees or caves. They use fire to cook their meat, and to use the language of DAVIS, their greatest "gastronomic" treats are the iguana lizard and roasted monkey.

Their language—if the few words they make use of can be called by that name—is a dialect of the Singhalese. The village Veddahs locate them-selves in the vicinity of the European settlements, on the eastern coast, living in rude huts of mud and bark, and are hardly more civilized than their brethren of the jungles.

The exertions of the goverment to reclaim this harmless but degraded people have in some degree succeeded, and a promising colony has been formed.

Ruined Cities of Ceylon.

In the north of the island, ruined cities—buried for ages in the depths of the forest—have been discovered, revealing monuments that in dimensions may almost compare with the pyramids of Egypt. The most remarkable of these vestiges of an early civilization is Pollanarrua, the ancient capital of Ceylon; and here is the celebrated Gal-wihara, a rock-hewn temple, supposed to be ' the only example in Ceylon of an attempt to fashion an architectural design out of the rock, after the manner of the cave temples of Ajunta and Ellora'.

PENANG.

Sept. 26th, 1875, arrived at Penang, or (Prince of Wales island), it is about 14 miles long and 9 broad, situated off the weti coast of the Malayan peninsula, in lat. 5 18' N., long. 100 4' E., ceded to the goverment of India in 1786 by the Rajah of the neighboring territory, Kedah. Area 106 square miles; population 61,797. The climate is healthy, and well adapted for the cultivation of spices, sugarcane, and tapioca.

During our stay at this port, some of our crew went ashore on liberty where they were kindly received by the natives, while in conversation with some of the business men of the place, they assured me that, the people are very much discontented under British rule, and consequently have frequent outbrakes in the island.

Singapore.

Arrived at this port Oct. 2, 1875, Singapore, India, is an Island, situated on the southern extremity of the Malayan peninsula. Its length is 27 miles, width 14 miles, comprises an area of 224 square miles, with a population of 97,214. The English took possession of it in 1819, since which time it has been governed by them. Sir Thomas Manning, is its present governor, who paid us a visit during our stay here. It is a great commercial and shipping imporium.

Passed Assistant Engineer Hunt, having been detached from this ship, left us to proceed to the United States.

Man the Life-boat!

Oct. 14. At 10. 30 P. M. the quiet and serenity of the ship was disturbed by one of the look-outs on the gangway, reporting a boat drifting by in a helpless condition, with a man in it. The Engines were quickly stopped, a boat was lowered and manned, but on reaching the supposed boat and man, it was discovered to be a large tree with out-stretched limbs, and birds roosting thereon, which screamed and flew away on the approach of our boat, as much as to say, we have fooled those Yankees this time.

Manila.

Manila is situated on the island of Luzon, one of the Phillipine Islands. It is governed by a Spanish Governor, who made a visit to the Tennessee, during our stay here, also the Spanish Admiral visited the ship to pay his respects to our Admiral.

Oct. 23. On leaving Manila, we encountered a very strong head wind which continued increasing in force for two days, so that it was imposible to steam against it, we were obliged to abandon our intention of going to Nagasaki, tacked ship and set course for Amoy, China.

A Wine Supper.

At 7 o'clock this evening, our Signal Quartermaster, Captain of the Hold, and "Jack of the Dust," gave their first Wine-Supper.

Amoy, China.

Amoy is a seaport town of China, in a small island of the same name, in the province of Fo-kien, on the sea-coast, is one of chief commercial emporiums of the east; and contains a population estimated at 250,000. It is divided into an outer and inner town, and has an outer and inner harbor, the entrance to the former of which, as well as the inner town itself, is strongly fortified. In 1841 it was taken by the British; by the treaty of Nanking, a British consul and British subjects were permitted to reside there. The trade is now open to all nations. The chief imports are rice, suger, camphor, raw cotton, cotton-twist, and British long cloths; the exports are tea, porclain, paper, grass-cloths &c. Smuggling is carried on extensively. Amoy is said to be the dirtiest town in the world.

WOOSUNG.

Woosung is a small village at the mouth of the Yangtze-Kiang river, 15 miles from Shanghai, is inhabited chiefly by Chinese, with the exception of a few Europeans who have charge of the harbor, there is one hotel, and it resembles all the Chinese towns I had the misfortune to see in regard to dirt and filth.

The English flag-ship " Audacious," and several Chinese gun-boats were in the harbor, who managed to make the night and day hideous, by saluting the Mandarins, and other Chinese officials, who are constantly passing up and down the river.

Nov. 23. Lieut. H. W. Lyon, left the ship in charge of the remains of the late William Seward, late minister to China, to proceed to the United States.

Pappenberg Rock.

At the entrance to the harbor of Nagasaki stands Pappenberg Rock, where the lives of so many thousands native christians had been sacrificed.

In the year of 1637, at Shimabara, the Christians rose by thousands in arms, seized an old castle, repaired and fortified it, and raised the flag of rebellion. Armies from Kiushiu and the Kuanto, composed mostly of veterns of Corea and Ozaka, were sent by Shogun to beseige it. Their commanders expected an easy victory, and sneered at the idea of having any difficulty in subduing these farmers and peasants. A siege of two months, by land and water, was, however necessary to reduce the fortress, which was finally done with the aid of Dutch cannon, furnished under compulsion by the traders of Deshima. The intrepid garrison, after great slaughter, surrendered, and then the massacre of thirty-seven thousand Christians began, and was finished by the hurling of thousands more from the rock of Pappenberg, in Nagasaki harbor. Thousands more were banished to various provinces, or put to death by torture. Others escaped, and fled to the island of Formosa, joining their brethern already there. The Edicts prohibiting the "evil sect" were now promulgated and published permanently all over the Empire, and new ones commanded that, as long as the sun should shine, no foreigners should enter Japan, or natives leave it. The Dutch gained the privilege of a paltry trade and residence on the little fan-shaped island of Deshima (outer island), in front of Nagasaki. Here under degrading restrictions and constant surveillance, lived a little company of less than twenty hollanders, who were allowed one ship every year to come from the Dutch East Indies and exchange commodities of Japan with those of Holland.

Nagasaki.

This is one of the snugest harbors we have entered duri ng our cruise so far. It is entirely land locked, and in the summer the mountains that surround the town are covered with green herbage , making it look very beautiful. I made my first tour in Japan yesterday, and will say that if first impressetons are the best I will certainly like the Japanese, I found them excessively polite, very obliging and honest, and their manner is so perfectly free from affectation, and simple, that I could not help but admire them, and of all the different nationalities I have come in contact with so far during the cruise, I much prefer the simple " Jap."

Our Christmas Abroad.

Our first Christmas aboad was passed most pleasantly, the day broke clear and pleasant, the sun shining brightly. The first thing on the programme was a boat race, between the Tennessee's barge "Magic" (12 oars) and the U. S. S. "Kearsarge" Cutter (14 oars), five (5) miles for $100 a side. The race had been much talked of in the fleet, and among the citzens on shore, the shipping in the harbor were crowded with spectators.

At ten o'clock the boats were out pulling around the harbor, at 10-30 the contestants came side by side, and at the signal from the officer in the umpire's boat (by the firing of a pistol) the boats started the " Magic" amidst shouting and cheering by the crews of both ships, took the lead and kept it, coming in half mile ahead.

A Christmas Greeting

TO THE CREW OF "KEARSARGE."

Long, long ago, (in memory's span   BY G. R. W
  It seems an age at least)
When Admiral Rodger's matchless barge
  Was champion of the East,

Her crew, as brave and strong a set
  As e'er a cutter graced,
Were wont to send a kindly word
  To those with whom they raced.

We envy not the Daring's fame,
  Nor boast her wondrous speed,
But only aim to act as square
  Whichever crew may lead.

And banish every petty care
  On this bright Christmas morn,
We'll do our best, come what may
  Our Bard shall blow our horn,

In honor of the gallant crew
  Who meet our craft to-day,
In friendly contest on the waves
  Of Nagasaki Bay.

Though one of us must be astern
  In this our maiden race
When each man does his level best
  Defeat don't mean disgrace.

Let's prove to others that the tars
  Who man Columbia's Fleet,
Are generous in victory,
  Or manly in defeat.

And cheer each other at the end
  What'er our luck may be,
We only wish both boats could win,
  Yours, truly,——" Tennessee."

The next event of any importance was our Christmas Dinner, our tables were decorated with flags and evergreens, and loaded with all the delicacies of the season, which we all enjoyed. In the afternoon a large party of the ships' company went on shore. Thus ended our first Christmas abroad.

The "Saco" Races.

The race between Admiral Reynolds barge Magic, and the U. S. Saco's twelve-oared whale boat Resolute, was closely contested for the first mile and a half, then the superior quallities of the Magic was plainly to be seen, notwithstanding the splendid stoke of the Resolute's crew, the Magic drew gradually away from her and turned the stake boat 40 seconds ahead, but in consequence of bad management in the turn she lost her headway, then the Resolute spurted and made a splendid turn, by this time the Magic got around and was off like a race horse, and finished a minute and a half ahead of her opponent.

New year's Races.

The first race with the Saco was hardly over when they manned their gig and tossed oars under our bow by way of a challenge to a six-oared race. Our gig like the Magic was untried, although built by the same builder, some of our boys were not so confident in her, but were willing to risk a little on her, while others speculated in the Saco's boat and succeeded in wining several small bets. The race at the start was closely contested, but our boat began gradually dropping astern and came in 50 seconds behind.

Having been beaten but not disheartned in this last race, our boys manned our dingy the smallest boat in the ship, with four of the bigest men in the navy, and tossed oars under the bow of the smallest ship in the service. The little ship won't surrender, the race to be pulled in one hour. The boats started over a zig-zag course around several men-of-war in the harbor, and ended in another victory for the Tennessee.

This race was scarcely over, when a short low rakish looking craft (not not of Ned Buntline's) was seen leaving the Saco, and heading right for this ship, but on closer inspection it proved to be her catamaran, propelled by shovels in the hands of four burly looking firemen, and on coming alongside demanded satisfaction their coxswain saying, "the little ship won't cave if you were as big as the Great Eastern, so get out your catamaran and if this don't turn the tables, we'll come over in a division tub." Our catamaran was speedily launched and manned by the Tennessee's Indispensables, and the race commenced, both coxswains wore very long serious faces, as if the fate of the Republic depended on the result, and kept continually working the body as if put together with a hinge in the back, and swinging their arms in all directions. There was great jockying resorted to in this race, running through propeller wells, under gangway ladders, mooring cables &c. Our catamaran the (lightning bug), came in several seconds ahead. The Saco's crew on leaving the ship was presented with a purse of Japanese tempo's and a wreath composed of onions, potatoes, cabbage, and artificial flowers. Thus ended our New Year's sports in Nagasaki.

Death of Charles L. Dickens.

Jan 29th, we anchored in the mouth of the Yang-tze-kiang River, for the purpose of having our quarterly target practice, the weather was cold and disagreable, we finished at five o'clock after two hours practice. The two boats that were sent to pick up the target were unable to reach the ship in consequence of a head wind and swift current running at the time, one of the boats drifting out to sea was picked up by a pilot boat and towed back to the ship. It was now eight o'clock, and just as we were about turning into our hammocks, when the cry was raised "man overboard," all hands rushed on deck, when it was found that Charles L. Dickens, a messenger boy, while standing in the port gangway slipped and fell overboard, all efforts to save him was in vain, boats were quickly lowered, gratings thrown overboard, but from the time the splash was heard, nothing more was seen of him. He was a native of Fulton Falls, N. Y., 17 years of age, a bright smart lad, and was a general favorite on board.

The following lines were written on his death, by George R. Willis, Flag-ship "Tennessee," January 30, 1876,—

IN MEMORIAM.

The bugle's tones ring out in martial glee,
The morning gun wakes echoes far away.
And, summoned by the notes of reveile,
We meet the cares of each succeeding day,

But there was one—the youngest of us all—
Whom duty cannot wake nor care molest,
No more he'll answer to the boatswain's call,
Nor can the guns loud roar disturb his rest.

For in the solemn watches of the night,
While darkness baffled those who fain would save,
Death, lurking 'neath the cold and angry tide,
Embraced our comrade in a watery grave.

Sweet be thy sleep, O, Charlie, thy sad lot
Decreed to thee a sailor's common end—
An ocean burial, and by all forgot
Save those who knew and loved thee as a friend.

But who would barter friendship's honest tear
For that proud woe which rank and wealth assume?
Thy mourners, though but few, are more sincere
Than those who decorate a royal tomb,

Comrade farewell! thy earthly cruise was brief—
We all must bow before thy stern decree
That calls us to attend a higher chief,
And ends our voyage on life's stormy sea.

The tide of time propells us swiftly on
To that dark gulf which you have crossed before
And sailing orders reach us, one by one,
To join the fleet that haunts the eternal shore.

Shanghai.

Shanghai is the second sea port in China of importance, is situated on the Yang-tze-kiang river, 15 miles from the sea. It is divided into four towns, the French, English, American or Hongkew. We are lying off American town which is the first town you meet on going up the river, it has not been long laid out, consequently has not as an imposing appearance as English town, it is inhabited chiefly by Chinese. There are as yet very few American or European residences here. The American Consulate and the Astor House, are the principal houses of European architecture. You come next to English town, and you 'are at once riding along a fine macadamized road that are kept very clean, the buildings are large, and built mostly of white stone or granite. The have one beautiful little park, in which there is erected a large monument to the memory of H. M. B. officers and soldiers that fell in the war of 1872. Next French town, which is smaller than English or American town, the houses are principally small and of little importance. You come next to the old original Shanghai City or China town, which is divided by a high wall, and while they do not invite visitors, you are free to enter during the day, but at night the gates are closed, and it is not considered safe for any Europeans to be found there after nightfall.

Division of Settlement.

The foreign settlement is divided into three quarters—the French, American, and English. These designations are given them for easy identification, and do not represent them as being quarters especially set apart for the location of the nationals whose names they take. Foreigners or Chinese can alike reside in any quarters they may elect.

Government of Shanghai.

The government of the place may be divided into two heads: the judical or paternal part, remaining entirely in the hands of the local foreign officials appointed by Western Governments, who deal with civil and criminal cases. The English Supreme Court is the only Imperial Court. The other Courts are Consular, with the exception of the Mixed Court. The Local Government, is carried on by Municipal Councils.

In the extreme south settlement the French have a Council, while the Anglo-American sections are managed by one Council. The first bears the title of "Conseil de l' Administration Municipale Francais," while the official designation of the latter is the "Council for the Foreign Community of Shanghai."

The French Consul, M. de Montigney, obtained in 1849 from the Chinese Government an assignment of space with which French subjects should be at liberty to acquire land and buy residences, &c.

In 1862, from an extension of the limits of the ground originally placed at the service of the French, the Consul established a seperate Council, which continued to administer its affairs under the regulations framed jointly with his American and English colleagues.

In 1868 a new code of regulations came into force, viz., the "Reglement d' Organization Municipale de la Concession Francaise," and the "Local Regulations and bye Laws," for the division of the foreign settlement north of the Yang-King-Pang. Both regulations have the same end in view. The powers to elect a committee or council to levy taxes at public meetings, for the maintenance of the peace, good order, and government of the settlement.

The regulations for the French side, work well. In regard to those for the American districts, the Municipal Council in their Report for the year ended March 31st, 1877, says:—

The affairs of the Municipality are in a prosperous state. The financial condition is satisfactory; the expenditure is 1,120 taels in excess of the receipts. This was to be expected, seeing the unlooked-for burden falling upon the funds during the year just concluded.

In Shanghai may be seen the essence of local self-government. They are however, laws to which foreigner and native are alike amenable.

The foreign councils administer the Municipal affairs. The are elected by the community. They tax themselves, and, although Chinese do not sit at the Council meetings, their interests are largely represented and cared for by an influential and wealthy class of foreigners, having considerable interest in Chinese house property.

On the whole Shanghai is the best laid out city, and the most civilized one, that the "Tennessee" has visited.

Chinese Holidays.

Yung-Chi.

A festival observed by all classes; it is also called Chang-shi-tsieh, or the time when the long days come, because then the sun begins to return, and the days grow longer. Officers go in state to worship the Emperor's tablet, and the people adore their lares.—Eleventh moon, twenty-fifth day.

Sie-Tsau.

The God of the furnace ascends to heaven to report upon the conduct of the Perfect August Shangti; hence people pay their adorations to that deity, sie-tsau, "thank the furnace." In some parts of China, this Shangti is regarded as the Supreme God in the Chinese pantheon, and it is supposed the other deities derive their power and position from him.

This popular superstition, though not peculiar to any one class, seems most closely allied to the taw sect.—Twelfth moon, twenty-fourth day.

Lei-Chung.

Festival of spring. This day, the period of the sun reaching the 15th degree in Aquarius, one of the chief days of the Chinese calender, and is celebrated with great pomp as well by the government as by the people. In every capital city there are made, at this period, two clay images of a man and a buffalo. The day previous to the festival, the chief city magistrate, goes out ying-chin, "meet the spring," on which occasion children are carried about on men's shoulders, each vying with his neighbor in the georgeousness and fancifulness of the childrens dress. The following day, being the day of the festival, the perfect again appears as the Priest of Spring; in which capacity he is, for the day, the first man of the province. Hence the chief officers do not move from home on this day. After he has struck the Buffalo with a whip two or three times, in token of commencing the labors of agriculture, the populace then stone the image till they break it in pieces, and many of them carry off pieces of the clay to put on their fields, under the impression that a better crop will thereby be obtained. Tho The festivities continue ten days in some parts of the country, but the ceremony attending this festival differs greatly in different parts of China, in Canton it is not attended with much display.

New Year

New Year is the only universal holiday in China. Other times and seasons are regarded only by a few, or by particular classes, but the new-year is accompanied with a general cessation from business. The merchant, and the laborer equally desist from work, and zealously engage in visiting and feasting—occasionally making offerings at the temples of those deities whose pecular aid they wish to implore. Government offices are nominally closed for about ten days before, and twenty days after, new-year; during which period none but very important business is transacted. On the last evening of the old-year, all tradesmen's bills and small debts are paid, and inability to pass this time of settlement injures a man's credit, and usually results in insolvency; while, too, the custom, by compelling an annual settlement of accounts, prevents many failures. This is perhaps the reason why it is called shu-seih, "the evening of dismissal."

First moon, first day.

Agricultural Ceremony.

On a fortunate day in the third moon, the great agricultural ceremony is performed at Peking by the Emperor and his ministers, and in all the provinces by the head officers of the Government. The ceremony consists in holding a plough, highly ornamented, which is kept for the purpose, while the bullock which drags it is led over a given space. The rule is the Emperor plough three furrows; the princes five; and the high ministers nine. The furrows are, however, so very short, that the later monarchs of the present dynasty have altered the ancient rule laid down by the predecessors of confucius, ploughing four furrows, and returning again over the ground. The ceremony finished, the Emperor and his ministers repair to the terrace for inspecting the agricultural labors, and remain till the whole field has been ploughed by husbandmen. The Emperor often appoints a proxy.

Twang-wu.

Festival of dragon boats. On this day many people race backwards and forwards in long narrow boats, which, being painted and ornamented so as to resemble dragons, are called lunchuen, dragon boats. From the narrowness of the boats, and the number of persons on board, there being sometimes from sixty to seventy paddles, it not unfrequently happens that several of the boats break in two; so that the festivities seldom conclude without the loss of several lives. The magestrates endeavour to repress the ardor of the people by issuing their prohibitions, but the people are led on by the excitement. The races are attended by thousands.

Empire of Japan.

Mutsuhito, the present Mikado or Emperor, succeeded to the throne February 13, 1867; was crowned October 13, 1863.

An ancient and extensive Empire, consisting of several large and many small islands, said to comprise in all 3,800, the principal of which are Niphon, (which in Japan gives name to the whole Empire), Sikok, Kiusiw, and Yezo. the latter being a colonial dependency, situated at the eastern extremity of Asia, in the N. Pacific Ocean, between 31 45 30' N. lat. and 128 40' 149 E. long. It comprises an area estimated at 155, 525 square miles with a population of 33, 110 825. Japan is said to possess a written history extending over 2,500 years, and that its sovereigns have formed an unbroken dynasty since 66 B. C., the present Emperor being the 123rd of his race.

Within the last few years Japan has made unparalleled progress in civilization and the adoption of Western manners and customs. The feudal system under which the country was governed by numerous lords has been abolished, and the Mikado is now absolutely the sovereign of the state. The Empire which was formerly excluded from intercourse with other countries, is now open to foreign commerce, consuls are appointed, and are allowed to visit the interior of the country under certain; almost nominal restrictions. The islands are eminently volcanic, and several of the summits are still eruptive; the chief of these Fusi-yama, the sacred mountain of Japan, a few miles from Yedo, is 14, 177 feet high. The country in general is fertile, indented with magnificient harbors, and the soil is productive, teaming with every variety of agricultural produce.

Foreign commerce is now being encouraged, and under treaties with several Europern States, the ports Nagasaki, Kanagawa, Iliogo, Ozaka, Niigata, Hakodate, and the city of Yedo, are thrown open to all nations. Capital Tokio formerly called Yedo.

Aspect of Japan.

The geographical position of Japan would lead us to expect a flora American, Asiatic, and semi-tropical in its character. The rapid variations of temperature, heavy and continuous rains, succeeded by scorching heats and the glare of an almost tropical sun, are accompanied and tempered by strong and constant winds. Hence we find semi-tropical vegetable forms in close contact with Northern temperate types. The aspect of nature in Japan, as in most volcanic countries, comprise a variety of savage hideousness, appalling destructiveness, and almost heavenly beauty. From the mountains burst volcanic eruptions; from the land come tremblings; from the ocean rises the tidal wave; over it blow the cyclone. Floods of rain in summer and autumn give rise to inundations and land-slides. During three months of the year the inevitable, dreaded typhoon may be expected, as the invisible agent of hideous ruin. Along the coast the winds and currents are very variable, sunken and emerging rocks line the shore. All these make the dark side of nature to cloud the imagination of man, and to create the nightmare of superstition. But nature's glory outshines her temporary gloom, and in presence of her cheering smiles the past terrors are soon forgotten. The pomp of vegetation, the splendor of the landscape, and the heavenly gentleness of air and climate come to soothe and make vivacious the spirit of man. The seasons come and go well-nigh perfect regularity; the climate at times reaches the perfection of that in a temperate zone—not too sultry in summer, nor raw in winter. A majority of the inhabitants rarely see ice over an inch thick, or snow more than twenty-four hours old. The average lowest point in cold weather is probably 20 Fahrenheit.*

The surrounding ocean and the variable winds temper the climate in summer; the Kuro Shiwo, the Gulf Stream of Pacific, modifies the cold of winter. A sky such as ever arches over the mediterranean bends above Japan, the ocean walls her in, and ever green and fertile lands is hers. With healthful air, fertile soil, temperate climate, a land of mountains and valleys, with a coast-line indented with bays and harbors, food in plenty, a country resplendent with natural beauty, but liable at any moment to awful desolation and hideous ruin.

Entrance to Yedo Bay.

To the right lie the two mountainous provinces of Awa and Kadzusa, with their numerous serrated peaks and valleys, which may be beautiful, though now they sleep. To the left is the village of Uraga, opposite which Commodore Perry anchored, with his whole squadron of steamers, on the 7th of July 1853. Remaining eight days at this place, he was accorded what he first demanded—an interview with, and the reception of President Fillmore's letter by, an officer of high rank. After the ceremony, he gave the place the name of reception Bay, which it still retains. Now we pass Perry Island, Webster Isle, and on the opposite side, Cape Saratoga. Now we pass the buoy indicating the spot where lies the U. S. sloop-of-war Oneida, which was run into and sunk by the British mail steamer Bombay, January 23, 1870. This is sad; but the sequel is disgraceful. Down under the fathoms the Oneida has lain, thus far undisturbed, our Government having failed to trouble itself to raise the ship or do honor to the dead. Little did the writer dream when passing the forts at the entrance to Mobile Bay, on the 5th of August 1864, side-by-side with the Oneida and her gallant crew, that he would ever pass over the grave of that noble little ship in Asiatic waters. The hulk was put up at auction and sold to a Japanese, for fifteen hundred dollars. This is the one sad thought that casts its shadow over the otherwise profound memories of which Yedo bay is so suggestive to Americans.

From serene and ancient Fuzi-yami the sacred mountain of Japan, we turn to behold the bustling upstart metropolis of the foreigners in Japan, as it appears in full daylight. Passing Mississippi Bay and Treaty Point, we arrive in front of what was once a little fishing village, but which is now the city of Yokohama. The town itself seems compactly built of low houses, with tiled-roofs. They are usually two-storied, though many of them are, in language of the East, "Bungalows," or one-storied dwellings. The foreign settlement seems to be arranged on a plan about a mile square. The Japanese town spreads out another mile or more to the right. Beyond the plains, is a sort of semicircle of hills, called "the Bluff." It is covered with scores of handsome villas and dwelling houses, of all sizes and varieties of architecture. To the left the Bluff runs abruptly in to the sea. To the right it sweeps away to the south-west. In local parlance, the various parts of Yokohama are distinguished as "Bluff," "The Settlement," and the "native" or "Japanese" town. Along the water front of the settlement runs a fine, wide well paved street, called "The Bund," with a stout wall of stone masonry on the water-side. Private dwellings, gardens, and hotels adorn it, facing the water. There are as yet no docks for the shipping, but there is the English and the French "hatoba." The former consists of a stone breakwater, or piers, rising twelve feet or so out of the water, inclosing a large irregular quadrangle, with a narrow entrance at one corner.

The French hatoba consists of two parallel piers of stone projecting out into the bay. The building of most imposing ugliness from the sea-view is the British Consulate, and near by it is the American. The Japanese Court house is larger than that of the Consulate buildings, and much handsomer.

French and English Camps.

At the other extremity of the settlement, toward the Bluff, was formerly the French camp, and near by it the English. Three hundred French soldiers guarded as many French civilians resident in Japan, and three hundred English marines, who relieved the Tenth British foot—the same that served their king on Bunker Hill— were in camp in Yokohama in 1875.

The Foreign Boors.

The predominating culture, thought, manners, dress, and household economy in Yokohama, as in all Eastern ports, is English. Outnumbering all the others nationalities, with the Press, the Church, the Bar, and the Banks in their own hands; with their ever-present navy; with their unrivalled civil service, which furnishes so many gentlemanly officials; and with most of the business under their cnotrol, the prevalence of English thought and methods is very easily accounted for. Because of the very merits and excellences of the genuine Englishman, the American in the East can easily forgive the intense narrowness, the arrogant conceit, and, as relates to American affairs, the ignorance and fondly believed perfection of knowledge of so many who arrogate to themselves all the insular perfections. Perhaps most of the Englishmen at the East are fair representatives of England's best fruits; but a grievously large number, removed from the higher social presure which was above them, and which kept them at their true level in England, find themselves without that social presure in the East; and obeying the " law of presures," they are apt to become vaporous in their pretentions. These persons are even surprised to find even American enterprise in the East. They are the most radical and finical concerning every idea, custom, ceremony, or social despotism of any kind supposed to be English. These men help to form the army of hard-heads and civilized boors in Japan, to which our own country furnish recuits. They the foreigners who believe it their solemn duty, and who make it their regular practice, to train up their native servant "boys" in the way they should go by systematic whippings, beatings, and applications of the "boot." Fearful of spoiling cook, boy, or " beto" (hostler), they spare neither fist boot nor cane. In this species of brutality we (believe the vulger John Bulls to be the sinners above all the foreigners in the East.

Tight-Rope Walking.

By kind permission of the officers of the U. S. Flag-ship Tennessee, Mr. and Mrs. Vertelli gave an entertainment on board Wednesday evening. Mr. Vertelli first performed on a trapeze suspended from the main to the mizzen masts, 50 feet above the deck, and asked if any one would volunteer to go on his back, when one of our men J. S. Peacock mounted the bridge and was carried across in safety, after which he gave an exhibition in magic, mystery, and ventriloquism. The men were highly pleased with the entertainment, and gave substantial evidence of their gratification by presenting their entertainers with a purse of $150.

The Missionaries.

Missionaries abound in Yokohama, engaged in the work of teaching, and converting the natives to the various forms of the Christain religion. It is a little curious to note the difference in the sentiment concerning missionaries on different sides of the ocean, Comming from the atmosphere and influences of the sunday-school, the church, and the various religions activities, the missionaries seem to most of us an exalted being, who deserves all honor, respect, and sympathy. Arrived among the people in Asiatic ports, one learns, to his surprise, that missionaries, as a class, are " wife-beaters," " swearers," " liars," " cheats," " hypocrites," " defrauders," etc., etc. etc. That they occupy an abnormally low scocial plane, that they are held in contempt and open scorn by the " merchants," and by society generally.

Audacious Boat Race.

May 12, 1877. The race between the barge "Magic" (14 oars) of the U. S. Flag-ship Tennessee, and "Albert" (16 oars) of H. M. S. Audacious, for the championship of the Asiatic Station, came off this afternoon. The " Magic" is a sister boat to the celebrated barge Daring, and of the two, is considered the better, She is built of oak and cypress, and was constructed by the builder of the Daring, Mr Hepenstall, at the Brooklyn Navy Yard, New York. Her length is 31 feet 4 in. and breadth not quite 8 feet, she carries a crew of 14 men; and while as buoyant on the water as a duck she is easily manageable. The Adacious boat Albert, was built on purpose for the Prince of Wales when he visited Canada, Admiral Ryder was then Captain of the Hero, the vessel which conveyed the Prince; and on returning to England presented Captain Ryder with the boat. She is built in three water-tight compartments, and is therefore a life-boat. Her dimenions are, length 36 feet 1 inch, breadth 8 feet 1 inch, depth 2 feet 5 inchs, weight two tons.

The present race was brought about through a challenge from the Magic and was fixed to take place at five o'clock. Much interest was evinced in the contest, both boats having raced before, though not together, and both being winners—the Magic having never been beaten. The Audacious barge was beaten once in Shanghai by a French boat, but carried all before her in Hongkong. Notwithstanding the roughness of the weather, quite a number of visitors congregated on the men-of-war, amongst whom was a fair average of ladies, to witness the contest. Others braved, the perils of the water, in sanpans and open boats submitted patiently to be tossed up and down and to an occasional sprinkling of salt water. As the hour approached for starting, the sides of the merchant vessels and all the men-of-war were lined with anxious spectators; whilst those who could not get a satisfactory view on deck went aloft. By half-past four o'clock both boats were manned and on the water, the Magic being under the guidance of Willis, with a crew of fourteen men. The Audacious barge had a crew of sixteen men, with Basant coxswain. Two finer looking crews it would be difficult to find. All equally stout, healthy and hardy looking fellows, it would be difficult for a stranger to say, with any correctness, which of the two crews was the best; and as the two boats lay, tossing about on the water it was not easy to distinguish which was the winning boat.

A strong north-easterly wind had been blowing all the afternoon, which was at its height by the time the boats were ready for starting, and consequently the water was very lumpy. Two boats were moored near the flag-ships between which were the starting and winning points. Finding that the preliminaries took rather longer than was anticipated, an effort was made to get the contestants away on equal terms by means of a line drawn between two moored boats, which, however, the high winds and roughness of the water rendered completly futile, and much time was lost in the attempt. At length it was resolved to start them without the line, which was accordingly done. The starter having got them well in line, hailed the coxswains, "All ready?" "Yes," was the response. The word "Go" was then given, and the oars dipped simultaneously. A wild cheer came from hundreds of throats on the "Tennessee" which was echoed from the "Audacious" and other vessels. Before the shipping was well cleared, the Magic had established a lead of a couple of lengths, and it was there seen that she cut through the water much cleaner than her competitor, who labored heavily and shipped a deal of water. The crew of the Audacious started on forty-two strokes to the minute and the Magic on thirty-eight. As they neared the light-ship, which was the turning point, making the course about three miles in length, the water became rougher and broke over the starbord bows of both boats. By this time the Magic had established a good lead; and it was plainly visible that she would give the other a bad beating. She turned Treaty Point four minutes ahead of the Audacious, and made for home at the same speed she had been going, still rowing thirty-eight and still increasing her lead. The crew of the other still kept up their forty strokes to the minute, occasionally rowing at forty-four. The Magic now had got nearly mile and a half of a lead, won the race nearly seven minutes in advance of her competitor. Deafning cheers greeted both loats as they arrived.

Lieutenant Goodrich, of the Audacious, acted as starter and judge; and Midshipman C. M. Winslow, of the Tennessee was Umpire for the Magic.

The following is a list of the Magic's crew:

Geo. R. Willis, Coxswain,

Edward Langdon,	William Clarke,
William Sutton,	John Campbell,
Robert Pattison,	Patrick Doherty,
Frank Smith,	John E. Sullivan,
Michael Sullivan,	John Chapell,
John Joyce,	Frank W. Brown,
Baptiste Charles,	Charles J. Cox,

The "Magic" is the barge of Rear Admiral William Reynolds, Commanding U. S. Naval Force on the Asiatic Station.

Fuji-Yama.

Kamakoura, fifteen miles from Yokohama—better known to foreigners from the proximity of the colossal bronze statue of Buddha than from any historical associations—is the scene of actions of half the romantic and heroic histories of the country. Huge temples, broad avenues, vast flights of steps, and stately groves of trees still mark the site of the ancient capital of Japan, are still relics of the days when heroism and chivalry went hand-in-hand, and when Dai-Niphon, "Peerless Japan," as her sons still love to call her, was alone in her majesty, and unknown to the world of "outer barbarians." North of Jeddo lies Nikko, the lovely burial-place of Iyo Yas founder of the Tokugawa line of Shoguns—a veritable" piece of heaven dropped on earth," a cluster of fairy temples set in a frame-work of some of the finest woodland scenery of the country. Away north again are the famous shrines of Ise, to which every Japanese who can do so makes a pilgrimage at least once in his lifetime. But all the pride and reverence of the Japanese are centred in the great mountain Fuji-Yama. The glory of the regular, pure-white cone, rising from the plain, and towering over the petty hills scattered to the right and left, has been sung by Japanese poets from time immemorial. Well-omened the house so situated so as to command a view of the mountain; fortunate the man who can show among his household treasures the duly signed certificate of his having made its ascent. Scarsely a screen, or a tray, or a lacquered bowl exists on which the well-known shape of the mountain is not portrayed. Ignorant rustics can not be convinced that there are spots in the world from whence the cone can not be descried. To the citizens of Jeddo it is a barometer, a protective genius, a sight to amaze the foreign visitor; to the peasant it is a something so sublime and grand as not to be spoken of without reverence.

The Centennial 4th July.

The celebration of the Centennial 4th July, was worthily observed at all the open ports in China and Japan. In Shanghai, a party of Americans engaged the steamer "Fire Queen" and took an excursion down the river to below Woosung. In the course of the trip the U. S. Consul Mr Meyers was called upon and made an excellent speech; and many patriotic toasts were proposed and responded to. In the evening the house of the U. S. Consul-General was thrown open to visitors of all nationalities, and the multitudes who availed themselves of Mr Meyers' hospitalities were welcomed with an open-handed heartiness.

At Chefoo the celebration was as marked as so limited a community could make it. A salute of 21 guns was fired in front of the Consulate at noon. A performance under the title of a ' Grand Centennial Performance was given by the Amateur Dramatic Club (not the Centennial Wanderers of the Tennessee) which did not break up until 2 a. m. on the 5th.

In Tokio, Japan, the Americans of Yokohama and Yeddo combined together to celebrate the day. U. S. Consul-General Van Buren, and a great number of Americans assembled at the Seyoken Hotel at Ooyeno and passed a most enjoyable time; while the "Tennessee" flag-ship of the Asiatic Station, had previuosly left for Kobe, a nice quiet little sea port in Japan, about 380 miles from Yokohama, where there are very few Americans, and much to the disapointment of the crew, who anticipated celebrating the 4th in a manner becoming an American flag-ship. No matter in what quarter of the globe one of our ships may chance to be, the "blue jackets" are always ready with their scanty purses as well as every other means in their power to help any person in distress, assist widows and orphans, or celebrate a National Holiday. On this occasion we had some difficulty in obtaining funds to carry out the intended programme. For this we can only blame our Executive in not doing his part (having the money served out). It was not until the very last moment had the neccessary funds been obtained. It had been raining for several days, and after waiting patiently all the forenoon for the weather to moderate, concluded to celebrate the day Rain or Shine. A splendid dinner had been ordered from shore, tables arranged fore and aft the lenght of the ship, decorated with flags and evergreens, and loaded down with all the delicacies of the season. Having done justice to the dinner, next came the Aquatic Sports, which presented the following programme.—

1776.  *1876.*

JULY 4TH.

Centennial Anniversary of American Independence.

THE CREW OF THE

U. S. Flag-ship "Tennessee"

Will chase each other around these heathen waters as follows:

PROGRAMME.

FIRST RACE.—3.30 p m.

Open to all Government built CUTTERS, excepting the Tennessee's Cutter-
Barge "Magic." Distance, about two miles, with two turns.

FIRST PRIZE......$20,   SECOND PRIZE......$10.

SECOND RACE.—3.50 p. m.

For Single-Banked WHALE-BOATS.   Same Course.

PRIZE......$15.

THIRD RACE.—4.15. p. m.

Tennessee's LIFE-FLOATS—Dreadnought and Dauntless,
Distance, 1,000 yards.

PRIZE......&5.

FOURTH RACE.—4.30.

MERRIMAN'S PATENT LIFE SUITS. Distance, 1,000 yards.

PRIZE......$5.

Winding up with a Race for the Championship of all Asia, between the
Tennessee's CATAMARANS Lightning Bug and Firefly.

PRIZE......CHAMPION FLAG AND GAME COCK.

Doors open at 3 p. m.   Children in arms not admitted.
No dogs or Jinrikshas allowed on the Course.—

Between the acts the "Tennessee's" Band played Airs and Selections by the following celebrated composers.—

Programme.

Tuesday, July 4, 1876.

Star Spangled Banner.

Centennial Hymn—.. .. .. Converse.

Grand March—"Kearsarge".. .. .. Murphy.

Overture—Le Cheval de Bronze .. .. Auber.

Waltz—Post-Horn .. .. Rossi.

Selection—La Grand Duchesse .. ..Offenbach.

Gallop—Wings of Love .. .. Meyder.

Quadrille—The American .. .. Marriott.

Waltz—The Duchesse .. .. Farmer.

Selection—La Fille de Madame Angot .. ..Lecocq.

Solo-Mazurka—.. .. .. Zikoff.

Waltz—Queen of the Roses .. .. Godfrey.

Gallop—Journey for Luck .. ..Faust.

J. Meyrelles,
Band Master.

On the following day the U. S. S. Monocacy, presented the same programme, having postponed the celebration in consequence of the rain.

Hakodate, Japan.

Hakodate is the most northern of the open ports of Japan, situated in 41 40' N. lat. and 141 15' E. long. The town stretches three miles along the base of a lofty promontory, which juts out into the strait of T'zigar, from the southern extemity of the island of Yesso. It is connected with the mainland by a low narrow isthmus, and separated from the mountainous region to the north by a plain bordered by an amphitheatre of hills. The adjacent scenery is striking and picturesque, closely resembling that of Gibraltar. H. was ceded to the Tycoon by the Prince of Matsumai in 1854. It was then a poor fishing-village, but is likely to become a place of much political and commercial importance. It is at present a small town with about 1000 houses of a single story, fragile wooden buildings with shingle roofs, which are retained in their place by coble stones. Each house has on its roof a tub filled with water for use in case of fire. The streets are between 30 and 40 feet wide, clean, and well drained, and macadamized. Considering the latitude of H., its climate is severe, and during its winter season the thermometer has been found to indicate 18 below zero. The snow disappears about the beginning of April (though it often lies on the mountains until mid-summer; and torrents of rain, brought up from the Pacific by the southeast wind, quickly deluge the recently snow-denuded ground. The harbor is one of the finest in the world, but difficult of access. The whalemen, who find in the neighboring seas a rich field for the pursuit of their calling, here obtain, at a cheap rate, supplies of potatoes, this important esculent having been recently cultivated with great success by the natives. By article three of the Treaty of Yeddo (August 26, 1858,) H. was, together with Kanagowa, and Nagasaki, opened to foreign commerce from July 1st, 1859. In 1869, Japan passed through a great political revolution, by which the office of Tycoon was abolished. In June, the Mikado's forces attacked Hakodate which was occupied by the rebels, and a great part of the town laid in ashes.

Alert's Boat Race.

Hakodate Sept. 27, 1877. A boat race between the gigs of the Tennessee and the U. S. S. Alert, was rowed over a three mile course, from a stake boat anchored in the inner harbor, to the light-ship and return. Previous to the race the Tennessee's boat was the favorite, having already won a reputatation in the East, and had never been beaten but once. While the Alerts on the other hand were willing to go their last cent on their boat, although an almost untried boat, having had but one race before. At the start the race was quite close the Tennessees's boat having a slight lead, on rounding the light-ship tried to hug it too close and lost her headway, and before she could be got around the Alert's coxswain taking advantage of the opening between his opponent and the light-ship, shot his boat through, slightly fouling the after oars of the Tennessee's boat, who claimed a "foul," but continued the race, comming in 20 seconds behind. The race was decided in favor of the Alert. The Tennessee's protested, and offered to renew the race which offer was declined until the other stakes were given up. This brought forth a "howl" from the big ship, "when the Mexicans like dirt, was sent on board the Alert, to founder that gun-boat completely."

Japanese Alarms.

Japan has been troubled by two distinct insurectionary movements, brought about by different considerations, and possessing no common source of action. The first was that the Samurai, or Shizoku: the second, that of the farmers. Fortunately for the Government, these classes have few interests, and still fewer sympathies in common. Both may, as in this instance, oppose government action; but they do so without combining. We might as well expect to see Thurlow Weed and Henry A. Wise stumping the states in harmony as the proud Shizoku and the humble Heimen uniting in opposition to their rulers. In the case of the Samurai the discontent was caused not so much by the new changes in their pensions, as was originally supposed, as by hostility to the Government for encouraging foreign intercourse. The old feeling against foreigners has been dormant for some time; but it exists, and grievances are looked upon as the result of foreign influence. In the case, of the Kumamoto riots, it appears that the feeling was not so strongly manifested against foreigners themselves as against the Japanese officials who support them and imitate their habits. The Samurai acknowledge the power of the foreigners; but they cannot forgive those who imitate them. These half-educated soldiers see no reason why Japan should be so rapily Europeanized, and they consider those who support such a policy the worst enemies of their country. And as a matter of fact, much of the distress and difficulty that exist in Japan is traceable to foreign intercourse. Rice, owing in part to the exports, has in many places doubled in value, and it forms the staple article of food with the bulk of the population. Gold coin, which was so plentiful, has almost disappeared from general circulation; and this is not unjustly laid to the charge of English trade. The decreased allowance of all the old pensioners of the country, though not so clearly traceable to the same cause, is generally ascribed to it, and the result of all this is that there is in Japan a strong party who hate the new regime and despise those who are at the head of affairs. The European dress and uniform, now almost universal with officials and military, is to them what the red flag is to the Andalusian bull. Careless of results, and without any definite aim, these Samurai rose, fought, and died. There was something grand in this small insurrection. Some of its episodes were very striking. In one place 190 men, inspired with a kind of fanatical patriotism, swore to kill an equal number of their renegade countrymen, or die in the attempt. How many of this band are now alive is unknown, but certainly most and not improbably all of them fell in the struggle or were executed afterwards, or themselves committed hara-kiri. The frenzy in some cases possessed their wives, who on the failure of the movement killed themselves. Most of those who, like the leader, Mayebara, were tried and beheaded, showed the greaest coolness and courage. They gloried in their fate, and used their last moments to upbraid their captors and deplore the fate of their country. The following is a translation of the "last dying speech" of one of the inferior rebels:—

A Dying Speech.

"Glorious country of Nippon, I am about to die for thee. Friends, let my head fall, my heart still beats for my country. I have not dishonored my ancestors; they will not reproach me. I join them without fear. I hate not the foreigners, but I hate the traitors of Nippon who suffer them to enter our land. Powerful are the barbarians, but we wish no trade with them. They cheat us with false treaties. Let me die a patriot; I have no fear. Like the bold-hearted Mayebara, I would rather die than live in a dishonored country. I am ready, Let the bold man slay me and I will thank him."

The Great Wall of China.

Another world-famous structure is the Great Wall—called Wan-li-chang (myriad -mile-wall) by the Chinese—which was built by the first emperor of the Tsin dynasty about 220 B. C. as a protection against the Tarter tribes. It traverses the northern boundery of China, extending from 3½ E. to 15 W. of Peking, and is carried over the highest hills, through the deepest valleys, and across every other natural obstacle. The length of this great barrier is 1250 miles. Including a parapet of 5 feet, the total height of the wall is 20 feet; thickness of the base, 25 feet; and at the top, is 15 feet. Towers or bastions occur at intervals of about 100 yards. These are 40 feet square at the base, and thirty feet at the summit, which is 37 feet, and in some instances 48 or 50 feet, from the ground. Earth enclosed in brick-work forms the mass of the wall; but for more than half its length it is little else than a heap of gravel and rubbish.

The Tennessee visited several of the most northern ports in China, and also anchored off Ning hai, a place where the wall terminates by running into the sea. Several of our officers and crew landed for the purpose of inspecting the wall, which is said to be one of the "seven wonders" of the world, and on returning to the ship, carried back with them, bricks enough to supply all hands with a piece of the great wall. On the return home of the Tennessee, each man will be found to have a brick (if not in his hat) most certainly in his clothes-bag.

The Heathen Chinese.

The population of China proper is estimated at 414, 686, 994: the dependencies, Mantchouria, 3, 000, 000; Mongolia, 3, 000, 000; Thian-shan, 1,000,000; Thibet, 11,000,000; Corea, 9,000,000, and Loo Choo, 500,000—a total population of 477,500,000.

The Chinese belong to that variety of the human species distinguished by a mongolian conformation of the head and face, A tawny or parchment-colored skin, black hair, lank and coarse, a thin beard, oblique eyes, and high check-bones, are the principal characteristics of the race. The average height of the Chinaman is about equal to that of the European, though his muscular power is not so great, the women are disproportionately small), and have a broad upper face, low nose, and liner eyes. Of the general character of the Chinese, it is not easy to form a fair and impartial judgment; and those who have resided long in the country, and know them well, have arrived at very different conclusions. M. Huc asserts that they are 'destitute of religious feelings and beliefs,' 'sceptical and indiffirent to everything that concerns the moral side of man.' As regards valor, their annals record deeds akin to the courage ef antivnity; they have no fear of death, commit suicide as the solution of a difficulty, and endure the most cruel tortures with a passive fortitude; but neither their arms nor discipline enable them to stand before European forces.

A Chinaman, has wonderful command of feature; he generally looks most-pleased when he has least reason to be so, and maintains an expression of imperturbable politeness and amiability, when he is sceretly regretting devoutly that he cannot take your life. Chinese cookery, in the use of made dishes, more nearly resemble the French than the English. Birds' nests soup, sharks fins, deer-sinews, and ducks tongues, amongst its delicacies. The wine, or weak spirit (tsew), more correctly speaking, used by the Chinese is made from rice; and from this, again, they distil a stronger spirit, the 'samshoo' of Canton.

Long nails are fashionable. The costume of the women differs but little from that of the men, and their shoes are the most remarkable part of their toilet. A lady's shoe measures about 3 inches from the heel to the toe. The feet of the Tarter women are left as nature made them, but amongst the Chinese, all young girls of the better classes are crippled by a tyrant custom. In early infancy the feet are tightly bound, the four small toes being tucked under the sole, of which, after a time, they become a part, and aud the heel is brought forward. The process is at length complete, stumps have been substituted for the ordinarv pedal extremities, and the Chinese lady totters on her goats feet.

A Japanese Theatre.

I went on shore early in the afternoon in company with my friend Perley, and took "Tiffin" at a well appointed Restaurant on Benten Dorie, where a pretty little Japanese girl named Kenosan waited on the table, and kept up such a lively conversation in broken English, Japanese, and Portuguese, that we did not put in an appearance until three o'clock.

In this country they adopt the plan of playing in the day-time. They often commence at 6 A. M. and go on until 6 P. M. The building was of wood, with a mean entrance enough. It was a large building, the part corresponding to our pit being unseated, as no Japanese sits cusomarily as we do on a seat, but literally on their heels. The floor was therefore simply matted with nice clean mats called tatami, made of straw and about two inches thick, so that they are soft and comfortable. The people leave their getas (wooden clogs, universally worn in the street) at the door, in charge of a proper person who gives them a ticket just like the attendants in the hat-room of our ball-rooms. They then go and take up their position on the mats quite independantly. The pit was divided into squares each capable of accommodating six persons. The stage occupied one end, a kind of gallery running along the other three sides of the house, divided into what I dignify immensely if I call them boxes.

The admission fee to natives was ridiculously small; but from us they exacted a rate something more than double the highest price paid by their own countrymen, and even then it was little enough. It was only two ichibus—Ichi-bu (one bu) is now as nearly as possible to a quarter of a dollar.

Having paid our money and entered the building, we met with a sight that, for the moment, dispelled all our notions of Japanese cleanliness. We ascended some rough bamboo ladder-like steps, and reached the boxes (as we will continue to call them); and being taken to one in the very best position, those who occupied it most obligingly rose to vacate it and make room for us. This we objected to; but they insisted, and so we were compelled to acquiesce; and made ourselves as comfortable as we could. There was no seats—only the matting as before described; but they brought a strong bamboo, and placed it across the box, resting the ends on the two sides, and on this we felt very much like the ancient niggar—"sitting on a rail."

The place was full; and as the curtain was down or rather un-drawn—for it does not fall, but runs along on loops from side to side—we had plenty of time to take a good look about us before the next act commenced.

As the performance is so long, and by day, most people were engaged in regailing the inner man. They can take their food with them; but generally it is supplied by houses specially connected with the theatre, the proprietors of which act as agents, and take the tickets, secure the places, provide the tabe-mono (food), give a written bill of the amount, and receipt when it is paid. The food is served in lacquered boxes in nests of four or five, the bottom of one fitting into the top of the lower ones, the uppermost having a flat cover similarly lacquered. These are beautifully made, and easily kept clean as the lacquer resists the strongest acids. There are no knives or forks every one using the chop-sticks.

The majority of the audience was of the softer sex; generally very nicely got up, their hair beautifully arranged according to the fashion of the country, and looking so bright and cheerful, that it did one good to see them. To our astonishment we saw in a box directly opposite to ours, an old lady with an opera-glass. My friend Perley, seeing her turn it on us, rose and made her a very polite bow, after the manner of the Japanese themselves; which so tickled her fancy, that she burst out into laughter; and directing the attention of all around her to our box.

Of the actors I am inclined to speak very highly. The seem more perfect than our own; and as they are thoroughly and exclusively trained to their profession, from their youth up, their action is wonderful. Like our own, their stage has its traditional tones, steps and gestures. and so excellently they do suit the action to the word, that although I knew no Japanese whatever, I could quite follow the sense of the play.

Altogether we were much interested and surprised with our first visit to a Japanese theatre.

Hong Kong, China.

Horg Kong is one of those islands called by the Portuguse "Ladrones," or "Thieves," from the notorious habits of its old inhabitants. The colony—which is described as exceedingly beautiful, possessing one of the finest harbors in the world, surrounded by lofty hills rising between 1,000 and 2,000 feet high,—was first taken possession of by Great Britain in January, 1842.

Hong Kong is thought by many to be an integral part of the Chinese empire, it is realy one of the numerous out-lying portions of the British possessions. The names of its principal street, its local government and a large part of its inhabitants are English. The history of its becoming a British possession is two well known, however, to allow me any excuse for introducing it here.

The town itself is situated on an island of that name, the straits between it and the mainland being only about a quarter of a mile broad. On the right lies the mainland, the chief objects in the landscape being the walled city of Carloon peeping over the ridge of gray hills, lower Carloon on the water's edge, and a bran new custom house. The aspect of Hongkong is singularly beautiful, as the position and plan of the city become clear to the arrival. Built on the steep side of a mountain known as Victoria peak, the whole place is laid out in terraces, the handsome houses, in clusters of trees and gardens of bright flowers looking like so many parterres in one large pleasure ground.

The steets are splendidly kept, and, with the profusion of trees, look like a carriage drive through a forest. Further up the hill lies the park, with a stream of water from the peak running through it and winding walks traversing it like a labyrinth. The English portion of the city is quite distinct from the Chinese, and its principal street Queen's road, is a broad thoroughfare flanked on each side by imposing public buildings. In the Chinese quarter, however, cleanliness is the exception. The houses are generally large, but crammed full of people like bees in a hive. But though the native and English quarters are distinct, many of the wealthier and English speaking Chinese merchants have their stores on Queen's road. In place of the Japanese jinrikshas, the Chinese have a singular conveyance shaped very much like a sedan chair, only instead of being borne in the hands at arm's length is caried cn the shoulders. These chairs are carried by two, three or four Chinamen, according to the distance or the weight of passenger. They are especially useful in a hilly city like Hong kong, where climbing the streets is a matter of great fatigue, and where horses could scarsely be of use. The legal fare is ten cents an hour, but genorarally grumble if half a dollar is tendered, especially if you are an American. All over the East there are two prices put on everything, one for the European and another for the American, the latter paying twice as much as the former.

Of course everybody who visits Hong kong makes the ascent of Victoria peak, so one afternoon, we took two chairs and started up the hill. The distance by road is two miles and a dalf and the height 1,700 feet. Agile and sure footed as the chair bearers are, they could only take us about half way, when we had to climb the rest of the distance. At the summit is an arrangement of flag staffs on which are hoisted the signals of incoming ships. Near it a lookout house fitted with telescopes, and as soon as a speck is sighted up goes the union jack; then, as the vessel nears, her nationality, and then her rig, and so on. A single piece on cannon and a miserable bust of the Queen complete the ornaments of the peak, which is little else than a high, bare rock.

Hong kong as in all British possessions, the inhabitants are poor, everybody is taxed from the Coolie Chair-man to the wretched boat-women that live in sanpans on the river, and subsist on the scum of the water. It is a sad sight to see one of those poor creatures with an infant tied on her back and three or four children holding on the side of the boat, waiting for the crumbs of hard tack that fall from our schute. This is the effects of British misrule in China.

The Centennial Wanderers.

January 1st, 1877. The "Centennial Wanderers" (Tennessee's Minstrel Troupe) gave an entertainment on board, which was well attended by both officers and men belonging to the English and German men-of-war in port, the audience numbering upwards of 1,500; people, when the following programme was presented:

MANAGER,	JOHN GILL.
MUSICAL DIRECTOR.	L. MOESLEIN.

PROGRAMME:

Aria Finale nell' Opera Lucia..........................Donizetti.

PART I.—MINSTRELSY

Introductory Overture .... Orchestra.
Opening Chorus, ... J. S. Peacock and Company.
My Love to all at home............................. D. Bowen.
Battle of the Yang-tsze-kiang, ... J. Gill.
Ella Rhee,...E. P. Wood.
Little Crossing Sweeper,"....................... W. H. Frazier.
Ups and Downs of the "Tennessee,".....................J. Gill.

Gallop..............Genevieve de Brabant...........Mallach.

PART II.—VARIETY.

Irish Character Song,................................J. Kane.
Song and Dance, ...W. H. Frazier.
Then comes the Important Question
WHO OWNS THE CLOTHES LINE!
Mr. and Mrs. O'Donovan,......................... J. Kane.
Mr. and Mrs. O'Hogan,.....................J. P. O'Donnell.

MAZURKA..............."ALICE"..........arr. by W. Erdmann.

Remarks on Intervention, ... Hon. E. P. Wood.
Echoes from the Rhine......................ED. Irving.
Excelsior Jig,................................J. P. O'Donnell.

QUADRILLE,.................. LA SOMNAMBULA..................Albert.

To conclude with the great moral Drama entitled,

A TERRIBLE EXAMPLE!

Or the mysteries of Temperance Hall.

Terrence O'Malley............(President).............. J. Kane.
Petroleum Nasby,............(Secretary).............. H. Long.
Labrador Leatherears ....:....(An Orator)............H. Church.
Squibbs.............. (The Terrible Example)............J. Gill.
Ilans,   ⎧ Members of the International Glee ⎫   ED. Irving.
Pomp,   ⎨ Club, with Excruciating Songs.   ⎬   E. P. Wood.
Teddy,   ⎩   ⎭   W. H. Frazier.
Landlord,.-.. D. Bowen.
Mrs. Bradly, ... J. P. O'Donnell.

ADMISSION FREE.   CHILDREN UNDER 45 HALF-PRICE.

Curtain rises at 7 30 p. m.

☞ Gondolas may be ordered to the main entrance at 10.45.   Long range Opera Glasses may be obtained from the Signal   Quarter-master.   Refreshments will be furnished from a well stocked scuttle-butt in the basement. No Peanut venders allowed in the Hall.

Bang-kok, Siam.

The King of Siam, at the suggestion of one our naval officers, requested Mr. Chandler, at the time an American citizen residing at Bang-kok, to prepare at his expense such a display as would do justice to his kingdom at the Philadelphia International Exhibition of 1876, and a very complete series of articles was accordingly brought together for the purpose. Owing to some difficulty, however, with the United States consul at Bang-kok, Mr. Chandler was arrested and imprisoned for a time, and the exhibit detained for a number of months. It has, however, reached San Francisco some time ago, and is now on its way to Philadelphia. The collection occupies 218 cases, with a bulk of nearly 1200 cubic feet. The entire exhibit has been presented by the king to the United States, and will doubtless in time occupy a conspicuous place in the National Museum at Washington.

Trip to Siam.

On the 4th of January the Tennessee left Hongkong, for Bankok, Siam, and arrived at the mouth of the Menam river Gulf of Siam, on the 11th. As the draught of the Tennessee would not admit of crossing the bar, Admiral Reynolds transferred his flag to the U. S. S. Ashuelot, and proceeded to Bang-kok taking, Admiral Reynolds and Lady, his Staff, and several of the officers, also the Tennessee's Band and Marine Guard.

One of the most wonderful cities in the world is Bang-Kok, the Capital of Siam. On either side of the wide, majestic stream, moored in regular streets and alleys, extending as far as the eye can reach, are upwards of 70,000 neat little houses, each one floating on a compact raft of bamboos; and the whole intermediate space of the river is one dense mass of ships, junks, and boats of every conceivable shape, color and size.

The vistors were cordially entertained by the Siamese authorities. In response to an invitation from Admiral Reynolds the King of Siam, visited the Tennessee on the 30th. His Majesty steamed down the bay in the Royal yacht, accompanied by a miniature fleet of steamers, on coming on board was received with all the honors due to his rank. The Royal party remained on board several hours, during which the crew was exercised at battallion drill, great guns, and torpedo practice. Being invited to participate in the torpedo practice he seemed somewhat startled, when, on placing his finger on the firing key, an explosion followed which raised an immense column of water over the ship's mastheads. His Majesty expressed much admiration of the excellent gunnery displayed by the crew, and when the target was shot away by Patrick Doyle, Captain of No. 13 gun, (11 inch pivot on spar-deck,) his majesty desired to see the man, had him brought into his presence and highly complimented him on his excellent shooting, also signified his intention of making him a handsome present. To this Admiral Reynolds would not consent, stating that, no one in our service from President Grant down to a messenger-boy, was ever known to take a present.

The yards were manned and royal salutes fired on his arrival and departure, and on leaving the ship His Majesty declared himself highly pleased with the various exercises, and paid his entertainers the marked compliment of describing a circle around the ship with his entire fleet.

The Tennesse left the Gulf of Siam for Singapore, sailed from the latter port on the 14th of February for Manila, having encountered strong head winds on the passage, called at the British Island of Labuan one of the Islands of Borneo, for a supply of coal.

Borneo.

Borneo next to Australia is the largest island in the world, is situated in the Indian Archipelago, and extends from lat. 7 4' N. to 4 10' S., and from long. 108 50' to 119 20' E. Divided by the equatorial line into two portions, nearly equal in surface, though of different shape. Its length is about 800 miles, a breath of 700, and an area estimated at 300,000 square miles. The population is variously stated, but the probable number is about 2,500,000. The coasts of Borneo, which are often low and marshy, and rendered dangerous to navigation by numerous islets and rocks, present no deep indentations, though they are pierced by numerous small bays and creeks. Of the interior, as yet comparatively little is known. Indeed, with the exception of certain not very extensive advances inland, made by Dutch and British enterprise from the south and west and north-west, the country may be said to be wholly unexplored. Two chains of mountains run through the island in a nearly parellel direction, from south-west to north-east; the one rising in Sarawak, gradually increases in elevation until it attains in its termination in Mount Kini Balu, on the north coast, a height of 13,698 feet.

Vegetation is extremely luxurient. Besides vast forests of ironwood, teak, the gutta-percha tree, ebony, &c. The animal kingdom rivals the vegetable. It produces elephants, rhinoceroses, leopards, bears, tigers, buffaloes, various kind of deer, apes, amongst which the erangoutangs are very numerous.

The population consists chiefly of Malays, Dyaks, Papus, Chinese, and Bugis. The Malays, who form the principal and most civilized part of the population on the coats, are very bold, but dangerous from their rapacity and passion for revenge. The are partly Mohammedans and partly heathens, and live, like their countrymen at Malacca, under sultan and rajahs. The Dyaks, dwelling more inland than the Malays, are unquestionably the aboriginal inhabitants of the island. They are well formed, yellowish in color, cruel and wild. They subsist by hunting, fishing, and piracy. Their poisoned weapons make them formidable enemies; but when their favor has been won, they prove trustworthy friends. The principal tribe of them is that of the Kayan. The Papus or Negritos are probably also aboriginal inhabitants; they live in the deepest woods and solitudes, in caves, and upon trees, naked, uncivilized, and seperate from the rest of mankind.

Victoria, Labuan.

Is an island of the Malayan Archipelago, situated off the north-west coast of Borneo, comprising an erea of 45 square miles, and possessing a population of 4,000 inhabitants. It was ceded to Great Britain by the sultan of Bruni, in 1847, being at that time unhabited; and a British settlement, was established in 1848, the first Governor being the late Sir James Brooke, The island has a fine harbor, and possesses extensive coal resources; but the latter have hitherto remained undeveloped, and the annual supply of coal up to the present has been altogether insignificant. The trade of Labuan, consists in collecting the products of the adjacent coast of Borneo and the neighboring islands, which are sent on to Singapore for the European and China markets.

On February 22nd, at Labuan, the Tennessee celebrated Washington's birthday. Governor Usher, who also act as Consul Gen. for Borneo, while assisting us in the celebration, the premature discharge of a gun caused the death of a native soldier. A purse of ($222) two hundred and twenty-two dollars was subscribed by the officers and crew, and handed to Gov. Usher, with the following letter from Capt. J. Young:

> U. S. Flagship "Tennessee,"
> Victoria harbor, Labuan.
> 22nd February 1877.

Dear Sir:

The officers and crew of this ship have heard with deep regret the accident that happened to one of your men while firing a National Salute in honor of the birthday of the Father of our Country, George Washington.

We deeply sympathize with his wife in her affliction, and beg leave to ask you to take charge of a small sum of money ($222) to be applied to the aid of the injured man, or his wife, should he die.

> I have &c.
> J. Young,

Governor Usher.

" Mr. Plunkett to Mr. Seward.

                    May 17, 1877, with accompaniments.

                                        Washington,

                                                May 17, 1877.

Sir:

        I have the honor to enclose a copy of a letter which the Foreign
Office has received from the Colonial Office, containing extracts from a
Despatch, from the Governor of Labuan, relative to the kindly feeling,
displayed by the officers and crew of the United States ship "Tennessee" on
the occasion of the occurrence of a sad accident to a private of the Labuan
Police; and I have been instructed by the Earl of Derby to convey to the
Government of the United States the expression of the appreciation of Her
Majesty's Government, of the sympathy shown by the "Tennessee's
company, on the occasion in question,

        I have the honor to be, with the highest consideration,

                            Sir,

                                Your obedient servant,

                                        F. R. Plunkett,

    The Honorable

            F. W. Seward,

                    &c. &c. &c. "

" Extract from a Despatch from Governor Usher to the Earl of
Carnarvon, dated 23rd February 1877.

        I regret to report that in saluting the American flag, on the occasion
yesterday, of the Birthday of Washington, Private Toviss of the Labuan
armed Police, while raming home a charge was, either through his own
carelessness in not properly sponging his piece, or through that of the man
serving the vent, blown away from the mouth of the gun, by the premature
ignition of the charge the deceased recieved such injuries that he died
within a few hours of the accident.

        I afterwards personally examined the gun, and satisfied myself, that
the mishap was not owing to any defect in it.

*   *   *   *   *   *   *   *   *   *

In conclusion it is necessary that I should report to your lordship the munificent conduct of the officers and ship's company of the American Flagship " Tennessee." By general subscription amongst officers and men $222 were collected for the benefit of the deceased police man, and handed to me with the enclosed letter from the Flag Captain. I must scarsely observe, that this, to her, a large sum, in addition to a small amount which I propose allowing her from Government funds, should place the widow out of want, the remainder of her life, and is greatly in exceess of what I should otherwise have considered it necessary to give her. But under the circumstances I was unable to decide to accept on her behalf, a charity so handsomely and unanimously bestowed."

The Fly Race.

While the Tennessee was lying in the harbor of Hongkong in January, H. B. M. gun-boat " Fly " happened to be in port, having the reputation of having a smart boat, the Tennessee's boys in order to make a stir in the harbor, challenged them to a six-oared race with our gig. The challenge was readily accepted by the " Fly," their boat being a shell built whale-boat felt confident of an easy victory. In the meantime the Tennessee left the harbor on an elephant hunt to Bang-kok, and the race postponed until our return. The Tennessee's gig being a heavy boat it was necessary to pick out a light active crew, and as fine a set of men as ever handled an oar was accordingly selected and went into practice, every one on board felt confident that if the race was lost it would not be the fault of the crew. When the Tennessee returned to Hongkong, we found the "Flies" all ready to light on the Yanks for a few Mexicans. A few days previous to the race, to the astonishment of some of us land lubbers who are not posted in matters of this sort, the crew was changed, and instead of the crew who had been practiced for the race, and stood the best chance of winning, were substituted by a crew of the heaviest men on board, which put the boat down to the gunwales, and left no possible chance of success. All this was known previous to the race, our boat had already gained the reputation of being "Pride of the East" was allowed to be beaten by a Britisher, a thing that seldom happens on this, or any other station. The race at the start was all one sided, at the word "go" the "Fly went off like a rocket, rowing a short quick stoke. Our boys seeing themselves astern, settled down to a long swinging stroke, but were too far astern to regain what they lost at the start, and came in 3 seconds behind, amidst great cheering by the Britishers.

In the evening the gig's crew were invited on board the "Fly" where they enjoyed themselves in true British style. "The British sailors rendered "Hail Columbia" to the music of a consumptive accordion while the Americans roared themselves hoarse in singing "God Save the Queen!" Toasts were drunk to the memory of Shakespeare and General Jackson, and the orator of the evening, (our Bow Oar) drew an eloqunt picture of the Eagle and Lion, occuping the same tree, and hatching their eggs in the same nest!" *

---

* It is realy too bad that (our bow oar's) memory could not be stretched a handful of years, when he could have drawn a different picture of those two loving birds, perched in the rigging of the steamer "Trent " watching two Secession eggs, (Mason and Slidell). Those times we indulged in another kind of boat racing. and no banquets.

July 4th, 1877.

The celebration of the anniversary of the Declaration of Independence in the port of Yokohama by aquatic contests, proved a decided success. Thanks to the exertions of the crew of the "Tennessee," who originated the regatta, and also to the crews of the competing boats. The weather was all that could be desired. A light southerly breeze assisted to cool the air, without raising a swell, which would have interfered with the rowing.

The first race was announced to take place at 3 pm., but, owing to the non-arrival of the guests on board the Tennessee, it was half an hour late. The fun commenced on board with the parade of the crews of the "Lightning Bug" and "Firefly" catamarans, who, grotesquely arrayed in nondescript costumes, preceded by fife and drum, marched around the decks, and then took their position in their craft alongside, where they were joined by the "Audacious" competitors, and a crew from shore, who were observed to have acted contrary to the rule on the programme, in that they brought a donkey and jinriksha on the course. These festive marine maskers contributed largely to the amusements of the afternoon, in which they were assisted by two Boynton dressed swimmers, who paddled about not unlike ungainly turtles.

Meanwhile the guests arrived, and the boats were placed in position in a line between the Tennessee's and Haydamak's sterns. From thence the course lay round the P. & O. buoy, across and round the spit buoy, and thence home to the flag-boat off the Tennessee's port quarter, a distance of one mile and three quarters.

FIRST RACE—3.34 P. M.

For Single-banked Whale-boats. First prize, Fifteen dollars; second prize, Ten dollars. Seven boats entered for this event. Shortly after the start, the Russians got a slight lead, which they increased to one or two lenghts on rounding the P. & O. buoy; and, although they were hard pushed by the two Tennessee boats, the Haydamak's crew won the race, amidst great cheering, by about ten lengths, the Tennessee's boat gaining second prize. Time 12 mins.

SECOND RACE—4.5. P. M.

Open to all Government Cutters and Barges, excepting the Tennessee's cutter-barge Magic. First prize, Twenty-five dollars; second prize, Fifteen dollars; third prize, Ten dollars. Ten boats started for this race, the Italians soon taking a decided lead, followed by the Tennessee's two cutters, going well, at a very quick stroke. At the P. & O. buoy the Italians were collared by the Tennessees, who pushed them hard with but half a length disadvantage. A foul, however, occurring between both the Tennessee's boats enabled the Russians, who were coming up, to challenge the leading boat. Rounding the Spit buoy the Russians had a slight lead, which they maintained, closely pushed by the Italians and Tennessee's. A splendid race down the open water between the Audacious and Tennessee ensued, the Russians winning, with the Italians second, and the Tennessee's 4th cutter third. At the finish, not more than a length and a half lay between each boat. Time, 11 mins.

3RD RACE—4.41 P. M.

Open to all Naval Gigs and Galleys. First prize, Fifteen dollars; 2nd prize, Ten dollars. Four boats entered for this race. After a good start, the English galley, pulling eight oars to their opponents' six, took a decided lead, which they increased at every stroke, and a rather run-away race ended in a win by any number of lengths for the English boat, the Tennessee's gig taking second prize from the Japanese. Time 11 ms.

FOURTH RACE.

Open to all Naval Four-oared Dingeys. One prize, Six dollars. Two boats started for this race, the Vigilant's and Tennessee's. When the men had warmed to their work, a slight lead was taken by the Tennessee's boat, and increased to six lengths in rounding the P. & O. buoy, and to ten lengths round the Spit Buoy, whence, having the race in hand, they won easily by about fifteen lengths. Time, 14 mins.

The starters for the above races were Messrs. WINSLOW and MARSHALL U. S. S. Tennessee; while Messrs. H. N. TILLSTON and S. J. ELDER officiated as judges.

After the fourth race was over, a race between the life rafts Dauntless and Dreadnought of the Tennessee took place over a course rather tortuous, winding among the larger vessels of the fleet. It resulted in a win for the Dauntless. Prize, five dollars.

A tub race followed, of three tubs, from the English vessels, the distance being the length of the Tennessee. Much amusement was caused by the efforts of their occupants to prevent a circular motion in these craft. The winners received a prize of five dollars.

Then came a race in Boynton swimming suits, three times round the Tennessee, and last but not least, the race for the Championship of all Asia between the Lightning Bug, Firefly, and a catamaran from the Audacious, the Lightning Bug securing the prize amidst roars of laughter provoked by the antics of their crew, who were composed of the Tennessee's firemen.

This brought the day's proceedings to a close, and many of the guests, it now being dusk, sought the shore, those who remained on board were regaled at a dinner given by the officers and crew on the occasion.

The night of the "Glorious Fourth" was as propitious to the revellers as the day had been: a dark night, with but few stars visible, showed the illumination of the "Tennessee," and pyrotechnical displays to the best advantage. The ebb tide assisted in swinging the ship's head northwestward, thereby giving a good view to the promenaders on the Bund. By a happy mixture of red, white, and blue lanters, tastefully arranged, the ship was shown in full outline, with ports lit up, the Haydamak assisting by illuminating her ports with white and red fires, which had a very pretty effect. At 9 o'clock the Haydamak's winning cutter filled with the men who had pulled in the races during the day, and tastefully illuminated with lanternes, pulled slowly round the Tennessee, and serenaded the officers and crew, with some very well sung airs to a peculiar accompaniment of Russian instruments of music. They were received with hearty cheers, and invited on board, where they were entertained to their hearts' content, a perfect feeling of brotherhood and good will existing among hosts and guests. Many of the crews of the English, French and Italian vessels, were also present and the general opinion was that they were having "a real good time." About ten o'clock the Russians took their leave amid deafening cheers and a display of blue lights, and soon afterwards the guests sought their ships and the shore, carrying with them a unanimous feeling of satisfaction at having enjoyed one of the pleasantest days ever spent in this port. We feel sure that all are of the opinion in according to the officers and crew of [the Tennessee a hearty vote of thanks, for the kind and gracious manner in which (while observing our national holiday) have provided such a treat to the community, as yesterday's Regatta and the day's festivities proved to be.

Miscellaneous.

July 28th 1875. Walter Lee Machinist, scalded by the bursting of a steam-pipe.

Sept. 18th,. great swimming match between John Cotter, and Henry S. Heath (alis Harry Gurr), the match was postponed in consequence of the water being too rough.

Oct. 11th, Passed Assistant Engineer Hunt, having been detached from the "Tennessee," left the ship for the United States.

Jan. 17th, 1876, half-masted colors, and fired 19 minute guns, in honor the late Vice President Henry Wilson.

Jan. 30th, The Tennessee enters Woosung river, and in swinging is stuck on a mud bank, The Harbor Master put up a sign "Keep off the grass?"

April 15th, The U. S. S. "Saco" left Yokohama, for the United States.

May 1, 1876. Samuel M'kibbon [I. C. B.] fell from the mizen-top overboard, striking the boat davit and broke his leg, was rescued from drowning by J. P. O'Donnell. This man deserves a Medal of Honor.

April 25th. The "City of Peking" on leaving Yokohama this morning, went ashore on a sand bar, off Rubicon Point. She is got off without sustaining any injury,

Aug 12, 1877, Rear Admiral Wm. Reynolds, and Lieut. Comd'r. Edwin White, left the ship to day, for the U. S. by "City of Peking".

Oct 3, 1877. Rear Admiral T. H. Patterson and Staff, arrived to day in the "City of Peking."

Dec. 4th, the "Tennessee" left Yokohama, Japan, for home.

Feb. 22, 1878, Hong Kong, China. Washington's Birthday was celebrated to day in a very appropiate manner. All the shipping in the harbor was dressed with bunting, a National Salute fired by the Tennessee, Monocacy, H. B. M. "Audacious," and guard-ship "Victor Emanuel." In the afternoon there was a boat race between the Tennessee's barge "Magic," and Monocacy's cutter " Shooting Star." Distance 3 miles, with one turn, for 50 dollars aside. At the start, one of the bow-oars of the "Magic" was broken, she went over the course with 13 oars, and won the race by four seconds.

Feb. 28, 1878. Death of Henry Long Fireman,—burried in " Happy Valley." The crew of the Tennessee, subscribes a sum of money for the purpose of erecting a monument over his grave.

March 2nd 1878, Rear Admiral Patterson, transferred his flag to U. S. S Monocacy, and the "home-ward bound pennant" is broke on the Tennessee, and weighs anchor for the United States.

March 13th, death of Michael Shaughnessy, [Marine].—buried at sea.

March 15th, death of Fredrick A. Crowley Ord. Seaman,—burried at sea.

April 15th left Aden, Arabia, for Suez, Egipt. Our home-ward bound passage through the Red Sea, contrary to our expectations, was one of the most pleasant during the cruise.

On the evening of the 21st, sighted "Mount Sinai," on the summit of which the law containing the "Ten Commandments," was given by God himself to Moses, amid the thunderings and lightnings and quaking of the Mount.

Near Suez, in the midst a sand desert, marked by a cluster of trees, is "Moses Well."

April 20th, 1878, arrived at Port Said, Egypt. This place has greatly improved in appearance, since our first visit, several large buildings have been erected, and other improvements can be noticed.

Alexandria, Egypt

April 27th, arrived at Alexandria. This city was founded by Alexander the Great. Its population once amounted to 600,000. The celebrated Pharos, or light-house, stand on a small island near the city. It was once accounted one of the wonders of the world. Cano'pus, near Alexandria, was noted for a temple of Sera'pis, close to it Nicop'ohs, built by Augustus in honor of his victory over Anthony; and in sight of this place, 1800 years afterwards, the battle of the "Nile" was fought between the English and the French.

Among the other attractions of Alexandria, are the Kedive's palace and Harem, Pompeii's Pillar, Cleopatra's Needle, all relics of former days.

Naples, Italy.

May 5th, arrived in the Bay of Naples, said to be the finest in the world. The city built on the side of a circular range of hills, present a very beautiful and picturesque appearance. The chief attractions here are: Mount Vesuvius, of the most active volcano's in the world, can be seen throwing up flames of fire and lava. Herculaneum and Pompeii, cities which lay at the base of the mountain, were both overwhelmed by an eruption of ashes and lava, A. D. 79. These cities remained unknown for more than sixteen centuries, but was at lenght discovered, Herculaneum in 1713, and Pompeii in 1750; the latter has been nearly all uncovered, and travellers may now walk through a great portion of this ancient town. It exhibits the full picture of what a Roman city was, habitations, temples, baths, the shops of the different trades, the implements they used, and even the material on which they were employed.

The King's Palace, Theatre St. Carlos, National Museum, St. Elmo Fortress and Museum, all of which well repay a visit.

Ville Franche.

May 11th, arrived at Ville Franche, a small village in the south of France, it is the rendezvous for the American fleet on the European Station. A large naval store-house has been built by the U. S. government, for the purpose of supplying the vessels on this station with provisions naval stores &c. About three miles from Ville Franche, which you can reach by carriage or rail, is the city Nice, a fashionable watering place for the European Aristocracy. The road which lead over a steep hill, which is studded with handsome villas surrounded by beautiful flower gardens, the perfume of whichs is so delightful and pleasant.

The ship's company get leave of absence for twenty-four hours, and, after spending three years among the heathens of China and Japan, it is not surprising that the crew of the Tennessee became so intoxicated with the beauties of "La Belle France," that they remained on shore several days after their liberty had expired, and in consequence, rewards to the amount of 2,500 francs were paid to the police authorities for their delivery on board, even then, it was not until within an hour of our sailing that all hands was reported on board.

During our visit at this port, there was a boat race between the barge and gig of the "Tennessee," and the barge and gig of the U. S. Flag-ship "Trenton," in which the "Tennessee" was beaten in both races.

The crew of the "Magic" present the "Trenton's" crew with a set of racing sweeps and champion flag.

The Tennessee visited Gibraltar, and Funchal, Maderia, where we spent a few days at each port, and the good ship Tennessee is headed for Columbia's shore, and is now pounding over the blue water of the Atlantic, proudly flying at her mast head the home-ward bound pennant 525 feet long, the longest ever flew in the world, where we expect to arrive in time to again celebrate the anniversary of American Independence, July 4th, 1878.

Ports Visited by the "Tennessee,"

PORTS VISITED.	DEP'T.	ARRV'D.	D'STNCE
	June 26,	July 13.	Miles.
New York to Gibraltar, Spain	1875.	1875.	3,250.
Gibraltar, to Palermo, Sicily	July 28,	Aug. 2,	914.
Palermo to Port Said, Egypt	Aug. 8,	„ 12,	950.
Port Said to Suez, Egypt	„ 14,	„ 15,	86.
Suez to Aden; Arabia	„ 21,	„ 26,	1,308.
Aden to Bombay, Hindoostan	„ 28,	Sept. 4,	1,646.
Bombay to Colombo, Ceylon	Sept. 11,	„ 15,	941.
Colombo to Penang, Malacca	„ 21,	„ 26,	1,288.
Penang to Singapore,	„ 30,	Oct. 2.	364.
Singapore to Manilla, Philippine Islands	Oct. 12,	„ 18,	1,389.
Manilla to Amoy, China	„ 21,	„ 27.	683.
Amoy to Woosung Bar, „	Nov. 3,	Nov. 6,	565.
Woosung Bar to Nagasaki, Japan	„ 24,	„ 26,	447.
	Jan. 27,	Jan. 30,	
Nagasaki to Shanghai, China	1876	1876.	459.
Shanghai to Yokohama, Japan	Mar. 30,	April 5,	1,058.
Yokohama to Yokoska, and back, Japan	April 17,	„ 27,	37.
Yokohama to Hiogo and back, „	June 5,	July 8,	696.
Yokohama to Hakodate „ „	July 26,	Aug. 21,	1,078.
Yokohama to Hiogo, „	Sept. 9,	Sept. 11,	348.
Hiogo to Shiminoseki, „	„ 11,	„ 12,	238.
Shiminoseki to Nagasaki, „	„ 13,	„ 14,	146.
Nagasaki to Chefoo, China	„ 19,	„ 22,	688.
Chefoo to Newchwang, „	„ 23,	„ 24,	157.
Newchwang to Taku, „	„ 26,	„ 29,	145.
Taku to Chefoo, „	Oct. 17,	Oct. 18,	203.
Chefoo to Hiogo, Japan	„ 20,	„ 24,	897.
Hiogo to Yokohama. „	„ 28,	„ 30,	348,
Yokohama to Hongkong, China	Dec. 17,	Dec. 28.	1,680.
	Jan. 4,	Jan. 11,	
Hongkong to Bangkok, Siam	1877	1877.	1,450.
Bangkok to Singapore, Malacca	„ 31,	Feb. 4,	807.
Singapore to Victoria, Labuan	Feb. 14.	„ 19,	870.
Victoria to Manilla, Philippine Islands	„ 23,	„ 26,	750.
Manilla to Hongkong, China	„ 28,	Mar. 3,	603.
Hongkong to Yokohama, Japan	April 5,	April 12,	1,680.
Yokohama to Hakodate. „	Sept. 23,	Oct. 2,	539.
Hakodate to Yokohama, „	„ 20,	Nov. 4,	539.
Yokohama to Hiogo, „	Dec. 4,	Dec. 6.	348.
Hiogo to Nagasaki, „	„ 9,	„ 10,	390.
Nagasaki to Woosung, China	„ 17,	„ 19,	390.
Woosung to Shanghai, „	„ 19,	„ 20,	15.
Shanghai to Woosung, „	Jan. 3,	Jan. 6,	15.
	1878	1878.	
Woosung to Amoy, „	„ 7,	„ 20,	600.
Amoy to Hongkong, „	„ 19,	„ 21,	280.
Hongkong to Singapore, Malacca	Mar. 2,	Mar. 13,	1,470.

Ports Visited by the "Tennessee,"

PORTS VISITED.	DEP'T.	ARRV'D.	D'STNQE
Singapore to Penang, „	Mar. 14,	„ 16,	364.
Penang to Colombo, Ceylon	„ 19,	„ 27,	1,300.
Colombo to Aden, Arabia	„ 30,	April 13,	2,200.
Aden to Suez, Egypt	April 15,	„ 22,	1.308.
Suez to Port Said, „	„ 23,	„ 26,	86.
Port Said to Alexandria, „	„ 26,	„ 27,	160.
Alexandria to Naples, Italy	„ 29,	May 5,	1,000
Naples to Ville Franche, France	May 9,	„ 11,	380.
Ville Franche to Gibraltar, Spain	„ 18,	„ 22,	775,
Gibraltar to Funchal, Maderia	„ 26,	„ 30,	610.
Funchal to New York, U. S.	June 1,		3.850.

Total number of miles Travelled by the "Tennessee"   44,788.

The following is the list of officers attached to and serving on board the U. S. Flagship "Tennessee," at the time of her arrival at New York July —, 1878.

List of Officers.

NAME.	RANK.
J. Young	Captain, Commanding.
W. H. Brownson	Lieutenant & Ex. Officer.
F. Hanford	" Navigator.
H. B. Mansfield	"
E. W. Remey	"
W. H. Everett	"
J. P. J. Augur	Master
W. A. Marshall	"
C. A. Foster	"
J. S. Abbott	"
F. W. Nabor	"
G. W. Melville	Chief Engineer.
J. C. Kafer	P. A. "
E. F. M'Elmell	Ass't. "
J. H. Perry	" "
J. A. Smith	Paymaster.
B. S. Mackie	P. A. Surgeon.
C. H. H. Hall	Ass't. "
R. Collum	Capt. U. S. M. C.
J. H. Sears	Midshipman.
C. J. Boush	"
E. M. Katz	"
A. E. Jardine	"
F. H. Sherman	"
L. W. Piepmeyer	"
W. L. Varnum	"
H. T. Mayo	"
B. Tappan	"
J. T. Newton	"
W. C. Putnam	Captain's Clerk.
F. C. Adams	Paymaster's "
R. H. Paine	" "
H. P. Grace	Boatswain.
E. A. M'Donald	Gunner.
G. W. Connover	Carpenter.
G. W. Frankland	Sailmaker.

The following is the list of the crew attached to and serving on board the U. S. Flagship "Tennessee," at the time of her arrival at New York, July , 1878, including a draft of invalids and others, from the European Fleet.

APPOINTED PETTY OFFICERS.

Richmond S. Davis	Master at Arms.
George R. Willis	Ship's Yeoman.
Robert Steene	Engineer's ,,
Thomas Glennon	Paymaster's ,,
Gustave Futterer	Apothecary.

MACHINISTS

William H. Trautman	Thomas Luscombe
William Holland	Dennis O'Mara
Walter Lee	William Lane
Henry C. Hume	John C. M'Guigan

PETTY OFFICERS.

Arthur A. Woods	William Sutton
Thomas Clarke	Frank Gillespie
James Mooney	H. W. Seaman
Francis M'Carten	J. P. Van Mendonck
J. H. Templeman	Thomas Harvey
John Foster	James Kelly
Richard Osborne	John King
Charles J. Cox	George W. Jones
William Clarke	Richard Maxwell
John Poole	Charles Carroll
Edward Langdon	James Cain
Patrick Doyle	James Gleason
Patrick Hurlehey	William H. King
William Fredrickson	John Chappel
John Leslie	Robert Pattison
Frank W. Brown	William Bray
Eugene Thurston	James Stewart
John Reynolds	Charles Williams
Edward Fogarty	Richard Scott
Samuel Erickson	James O. House
Michael Woods	Frank Pourhine

William Darby
Thomas M'Carthy
John V. Fawcett
William A. Pratt
Michael Walsh
James Tinney

Charles M. Smith
John Campbell
James C. Robinson
Patick Doherty
John Williams

SEAMEN

Charles Brinkerhoff
Thomas Harms
William J. Duncan
Mayakwa Minetara
John E. Bell
William M'Farland
John Doherty
John K. Wilson
William A. Arey
Robert Andrews
George Cronin
Henry Cader
Thomas Dyer
Joseph Holmes
Charles Fields
Patrick Fitzgerald
David Fleming
James Ingalls
John Johnson
Herman Johnson
Edward Jackson
Charles J. Meyers
Robert Kenchington
William Smith
John Anderson
Thomas Powell
Frank Riley
John W. Anderson
John Farwell
John Brittney
James Rowan
John Rowley
Philip Moore
Henry Smith
John E. Sullivan
Charles Smith
John Thompson
Thomas Malcolm
John B. Mitchell
Charles H. Wooley
Charles Williams

Charles Ahl
William Butler
William Eske
Alonzo Cross
William H. Cosgroye
Nath'l Carllson
George R. Baker
Edward J. Carroll
John Barry
Joseph Childs
Jeremiah Creamer
Robert Kelly
Henry Jones
Michael Collins
Fredrick Danitz
John Long
Steward M'Mullins
Carl Muller
Daniel M'Gonagle
Charles Pieplow
Michael M'Glade
John Neill
Gustat Smith
Charles G. Smith
Edward Warren
Jeremiah Murphy
John Anderson
Baptist Charles
William Lindemer
Patrick Regan
James E. Donahoe
George H. Kraemer
Charles H. Nichols
Frank Smith
John M'Keon
Samuel Reading
John Lyons
Peter Nelson
William Brown
William Johnson

P.P. SEAMEN, LANDSMEN &c.

William Ashcroft
Hendrk Booland
Daniel Bowen
Charles Beekman
William Costello
Thomas Coleman
J. G. L. Castelaino
Daniel Crowley
Edward Davis
John Doherty
James J. Easton
Christopher Kinsley
John Lickfield
William O'Donnell
John P. O'Donnell
James S. Peacock
William T. Proudfoot
William Rasmus
Richard Riley
Mathew Reilley
Edward C. Goff
Eugene Sullivan
James M'Guire
William Davidson
Edward Woods
William C. Pennington
William T. Simon
Charles Sinclair
Edwin H. Bush
George Speckman
Michael Sullivan
J. A. Samuelson
John M'Carteny
Griffith M. Copper
James Do'l'ng
Hugh Brown
Edward Brennen
August Buman
Henry Church
John Cotter
John E. Doyle
Jeremiah Driscoll
Arnold Ritz
Andrew J. Farrell
Charles L. Frailey
Bartlett Goland
John M'Lelland
Godfrey Lodge
C. N. Thompson
Thomas Clarke
Lucius P. Bacon
Franz Schmidt
William J. Corcoran

James Elliott
Arthur B. Friend
Joseph Frank
George Grieves
John Grant
John Graham
William Goodman
Henry S. Heath
John P. Johnson
Coleman Flaherty
Fritz Jacobs
Michael Sweeney
George E. Davis
William C. Towen
Frank B. Whitman
John J. Walton
James Wilson
Daniel Lyons
Samuel M'Kibbon
Thomas J. M'Cormack
William Murphy
John Daniels
Francis P. Wryeon
Ferdinand Sceeve
Michael Dunn
William H. Dobbs
Timothy M'Namara
Antonio Munoz
Charles P. Phillips
John Joyce
William Hampton
Albert J. Kennedy
Daniel Maher
Jacob O. Thompson

John Griffin
Martin Howley
Robert H. Hatch
Charles Hubbard
William Harrison
Albert Herzberger
James Keenan
John J. Leary
Patrick Meers
William H. Marsh
James Murphy
Henry Snedicor
Thomas Darwin
Charles Costello
Eugene D. Sullivan
Nelson Homes
George W. White
Jacob Weborg

Frank Mulligan
Terrence M' Sweeny
Lewis Gales
George Phillips
Frank Leslie
Charles Subold
Edgar Frazier
Harry Jackson
Axal Vanneistrom
Clarence J. Tubbs
William Edwards
Austin Davis
J. B. Norwood
Jessie Lippey
Thomas Parker
Claude Du Quoin
J. W. Cromwell
William Hollingsworth
William Sheppard

John Campbell
H. C. Ellis
James Flemming
W. A. Anderson
Henry T. Carson
J. M. Beam
Thomas Bell
Owen Brennen
William C. Bennett
William Little
William F. Watkins
J. H. Wayson
Rosely T. Holt
B. Muraoka
Yosuke Mosuka.
Hudson Phillips
David Sunford.
James Long

FIREMEN.

Charles Doherty
James Connor
Peter Farrell
James M'Cormack
Solomon W. Bowdy
Albert Bossing
James Butler
John Bates
Patrick Cronin
James Moore
John Mooney
James Roache
Joseph Travers
John B. Stephens
Jeremiah Shea
Christian Christiansen.
Thomas Q. Karr
Richard Bennett
Patrick Carroll
James Crassen
William H. Frazier
John E. Gallagher
Robert Hughes
Daniel Handly
John Kane
John O'Neil
John Carlson
John Wilson,

William Murray
Patrick Phillips
Edward Quirk
William Riley
William Rankin
William Taylor
John Tobin
Frank B. Frost
Thomas White
Robert M'Kenzie
John F. M'Adams
Edward Irving
Thomas H. Simmons
John Sharpe
Edward Toomey
Peter Melvey
William Warwick
William C. C. Meyer
John F. Mariani
George Knoll
John Wilson
Julius Jensen
Peter Hess
Francis Connolly
John Walsh
Patrick M'Donnald
Ezia L. Mead
Miles Parel

MARJNES·

Frank Neiderreuther	Ord. Sergt.	Thomas Gaskin	Private
James Ray	Sergt.	Phillip Hoyle	,,
George Rousell	,,	Edward Kensett	
Frank C. Neipman	,,	William H. Knight	
Corneilus Whelton	Corporal	Thomas Landy	
John A. Casey	,,	John Lee	
Henry Landgrebe	,,	Robert Lamar	
James Dougherty	,,	Frank Moran	
John A. Scrivener	Drummer	Patrick Murphy	
Irvine N. Wharton	Fifer	Thomas M'Nally	
Henry Bender	Private	Daniel M'Clellan	
Michael Brady	,,	Hugh M'Court	
James B. Cölt	,,	John O'Leary	
John Carlin	,,	Charles Jones	
Thomas Daniels		Joseph E. Randolph	
James K. Dawson		William W. Smith	
Maurice Desmond		Frank Steinhouse	
Francis J. Deisenrott		Frederick Shelp	
Henry Fisher		Charles B. Walsk	
Richard Finnegan		Joseph Young	

MUSJPJANS.

Joakin Meyrelles	Leader	Otto Peterson
William C. Egan		John Reinhardt
John Stephen		Augustine Audiberti
John Fitch		Achille Jedesche
James Glenny		Domenico Zito
Thornhill Percival		Giacomo Rinaldi
Frederick Fronfeldt		Errico Forti
William G. B. Erdman		Giussippe Allessio
John Johnson		Eugene Millo
Leopold Moselein		John Kollmer

THE PRINTER'S TROUBLES

When the Tennessee visited Ville Franche, Rear Admiral Le Roy, then Commanding U. S. Naval Force on the European Station, paid a visit to the "Tennessee," on going around inspecting the ship asked to be shown to the Printing Office. he said his ship the "Trenton" was fited out with all the modern inventions, Roache's compound treble back-acting engines, Converted rifles, fired by electricity, patent gun-carriages, steam steering apparatus &c., and regretted to say that they were at least a Century behind the age in in a Printing Press, but had been told that the "Tennessee" had a "lightning press" on board, and asked to see it. He was shown to the printing office where he was received by the "printer's devil" whom he recognized as one of the party who went to his assistance one morning he was caught napping on the blockade, when he Commanded the "Keystone State" off Charleston, S. C. on the morning of the 31st, of January 1863, when attacked by the Confederate ram "Palmetto State," and knocked into a cocked hat, when he headed sea-ward like a crab with one wheel out of water. The Admiral like all other naval officers give very little credit to the "blue-jackets" who have stood by their guns in time of need, and elevating his eye-glass the same pair he wore when attacked by the ram, as was seen to be minus one of the glasses, demanded to see the "lightning press," when the "devil" pointed to something resembling a Nut Cracker which stood in a dark corner on the berth-deck, he laughed heartily when shown a copy of the Cruise of the Tennessee then on the press, and immediately gave orders to have the whole business sent on board the "Trenton" which was accordingly done, notwithstanding the protest of the "devil" who said he intended to have the piratical act investigated. Consequently I am compelled to bring this little book to a close.

In consideration of the great disadvantages in which this little work has been printed, the reader is requested to over-look several typographical errors, as it has been got up merely for the purpose of breaking the monotony of this tedious cruise.

Very Respectfully
Yours &c.,
F. M'Carten.

THE OLD PRINTING PRESS.

A song to the Press, the Tennessee's Press!
  Of the good old-fashioned kind,
Ere the giant machine, with its pulse of steam,
  Elbows it out of mind.
  In the days of yore
  Our fathers hoar
    By his sturdy limbs have wrought
  Of iron or oak,
  His teachings spoke,
    The language of burning thought.

A song to the Press, the Tennessee's Press!
  As the carriage rolls merrily along,
His old sides groan, as the bar pulls home,
  Keeping time to the pressman's song
  And the crisp, wet sheet
  On its errand fleet
    By anxious hands is sped
  Though oft elsewhere
  It may sorrow bear,
    It brings the printer (10 ounces) of bread.

U. S. S. "Tennessee,"
July 5, 1878.